Charles Neidhard

Crotalus Horridus

its analogy to yellow fever, malignant, bilious, and remittent fevers,

demonstrated by the action of the venom on man and animals

Charles Neidhard

Crotalus Horridus
*its analogy to yellow fever, malignant, bilious, and remittent fevers, demonstrated
by the action of the venom on man and animals*

ISBN/EAN: 9783337382650

Printed in Europe, USA, Canada, Australia, Japan

Cover: Foto ©Andreas Hilbeck / pixelio.de

More available books at **www.hansebooks.com**

CROTALUS HORRIDUS.

ITS ANALOGY TO

YELLOW FEVER,

MALIGNANT, BILIOUS, AND REMITTENT FEVERS.

DEMONSTRATED BY THE ACTION OF THE VENOM ON MAN
AND ANIMALS.

WITH AN ACCOUNT OF HUMBOLDT'S PROPHYLACTIC INOCULATION OF THE
VENOM OF A SERPENT, AT HAVANA, CUBA.

BY C. NEIDHARD, M.D.,

LATE PROFESSOR OF CLINICAL MEDICINE IN THE HOMŒOPATHIC MEDICAL COLLEGE OF PENNSYLVANIA, ORDINARY AND CORRESPONDING MEMBER OF THE HOMŒOPATHIC SOCIETIES OF LEIPZIG, PARIS, VIENNA, &C., &C.

SECOND EDITION, REVISED AND ENLARGED.

NEW-YORK:

WM. RADDE, No. 550 PEARL-STREET.

PHILADELPHIA: F. E. BOERICKE, 635 Arch-st.

Boston: OTIS CLAPP.—St. Louis: H. C. G. LUYTIES.—Cincinnati: SMITH & WORTHINGTON.—Detroit: E. A. LODGE, M.D.—Chicago: C. S. HALSEY.—Cleveland: BECKWITH & Co.—Pittsburg, Pa.: J. G. BACKOFEN & SON.—London, Eng.: H. TURNER & Co., No. 77 Fleet Street; JAMES EPPS, No. 112 Great Russell Street.

1868.

PREFACE.

The following account of the Yellow Fever in Philadelphia, during the year 1853, was written at the time of its occurrence. Some cases of Bilious Remittent Fever were added subsequently. The facts seemed to me important enough to be preserved in the archives of homœopathy.

My almost exclusive use of CROTALUS in the milder cases of this otherwise formidable disease was involuntary. I prescribed it, again and again, because it was the only remedy which seemed most promptly to subdue the symptoms of this disease.

On comparing the pathogenetic effects of CROTALUS, from MURE, HERING, and JAHR, with the prominent phenomena of Yellow Fever, the conviction cannot fail to impress itself upon the reader's mind, as it did upon mine, that CROTALUS *is probably the principal, if not the only true homœopathic remedy, even in the more formidable cases of this disease.*

This is farther corroborated by the prophylactic inoculation of the same agent, instituted by HUMBOLDT in the military hospital at Havana. Farther experience in the South, on a large and extended scale, will be required to confirm or overthrow this supposition.

THE AUTHOR.

PREFACE TO THE SECOND EDITION.

In this preface to his second edition, the author wishes to draw the attention of the medical public to the remarkable and exhaustive work of *Dr. S. W. Mitchell, on the venom of the Crotalus Horridus*, wherein his own views are fully confirmed. *Dr. Mitchell considers the effect of the venom of the rattle-snake, and that of the Yellow Fever, on the human body as almost identical.* His views are the more to be credited as coming from an author who does not believe in the efficacy of the poison, if internally administered, as mentioned in the works of Fontana, Jeter, Burnett and others, as well as the whole homœopathic school. Neither is he an advocate of the homœopathic law of cure.

The candid inquirer after reading the observations of Dr. Mitchell cannot fail of arriving at the conclusion, that the venom of the Crotalus is the true specific, or homœopathic remedy in Yellow Fever, as well as in similar fevers. This similarity manifests itself not merely by external symptoms, (surface symptomatology) but by the deeper action on the nervous centres and the blood. In other words, the symptoms of the Yellow Fever poison, as well as those of the Crotalus poisoning, may, according to the individuality of the person afflicted, vary with this individuality; all drug as well as natural diseases, most easily affecting the weakest organs; but in their grand general features both poisons will be found wonderfully analogous to each other.

Yellow Fever being only an aggravated form of Malignant Bilious Fever, we have, for this reason, found Crotalus so useful in the latter disease.

TABLE OF CONTENTS.

NOTICES OF THE PRESS, &c.

This work undoubtedly calls for a special notice by the Homœopathic Press, as well as in consequence of its issuing from the able pen of one of our most scientific and successful practitioners of homœopathy, as on account of the high practical importance of its contents. * * * * * To judge from these facts there cannot, for all those that are familiar with the fundamental law of nature in curing disease be any doubt, that *Crotalus Horridus*, if it is not the specific for Yellow Fever and its kindred diseases * * * must at least become the most efficient means to reduce the deadly virulence of that malady.

We recommend Dr. Neidhard's work to the careful perusal of all that take interest in the cause of humanity, medical science and human art particularly. Almost every one may learn something by it, and our brethren of the old school (supposing they were willing to learn), might by studying it, get a glimpse of the truth, that the great principle of homœopathy, *similia similibus curantur*, is an invariable law of nature, which even the most foolishly conducted experiments (as was the case in the Military Hospital in Cuba) will bring to light.—*U. S. Journal of Homœopathy, Feb.* 1860.

A valuable monograph upon a remedy which, relatively, is new to the profession. If the author be not altogether too sanguine, we may expect the best results to come of its general use by Western and Southern physicians in the graver forms of bilious remittent fever, to say nothing of that scourge, the Yellow Fever, should it again prevail on our shores. He certainly makes out a very good case, and it were worth our while to test the matter, and know if it be possible, by such means, to cure a violent fever, which often lasts from five to six weeks, in the short space of a fortnight. We append the table of contents premising that Chapter VI. and VII. are more interesting than aught contained in the *Atlantic* or *Harper* for November.—*Medical Investigator, Chicago.*

"Dr. Neidhard makes a comparison of the symptoms of Yellow Fever with those produced by the bite of the rattlesnake (Crotalus Horridus), and, imperfect as is our knowledge of the pathogenetic effects of this virus, the disease seems to be pretty well represented in its symptomatology, thus justifying his belief, that Crotalus is truly homœopathic in Yellow Fever.

It seems evident, that the inoculation produced a well-defined group of symptoms, closely resembling those of Yellow Fever, and we consider *Dr. Neidhard justified in pronouncing it a truly homœopathic remedy in the disease, and we can understand his successful employment of it.*"—*British Journal of Homœopathy, Vol.* 15, *page* 468

One of our most esteemed colleagues furnished his experience on a subject which is of the greatest importance to suffering humanity, as well as medical science.

From the copious extracts, which we have made from the work, it will be seen, that it contains a rich material of the most interesting and important data, well worthy of farther investigation. We recommend it therefore to all those who are acquainted with the English language.

Dr. Neidhard's experience may not be sufficient to prove Crotalus, the specific remedy in Yellow Fever, but every practitioner must be indebted to our author for the valuable communication of his experience, by which the severe sufferings of these diseases can be relieved much better, than was possible hitherto by other remedies.—*Neue Zeitschrift für Hom. Klinik, von Dr. B. Hirschel in Dresden.*

The value of Crotalus in bilious or yellow fevers is confirmed by the extracts from the works of Mure and Jahr, which show the symptoms of this poison as strikingly similar to the phenomena of Yellow Fever and the more malignant cases of bilious fever. * * * The details are full of interest, not only to the profession but to the general reader. Dr. N. deservedly enjoys a high reputation in this city.—*Philadelphia Inquirer.*

A Spanish translation of the work has appeared in Barcelona, and is for sale in Havana, Cuba, at "Imprenta y Liberia de Dr. D. Andres Graupera, calle del Obispo No. 113. The following is the Spanish Preface.

"Habiendo Negado á mis manos el interesante opusculo que publicó el ano pasado, en Nueva York, M. C. Neidhard, Doctor en Medicina, sobre la eficacia del virus de la Serpiente cascabel (Crotalus Horridus) para la curacion de la fiebre amarilla, he creido que no podia menos de ser bien recibida su traduccion al castellano por el Público de esta grande Autilla, centro importante de tan vasto comercio entre Europa y America, y á donde acuden tantos peninsulares y estrangeros, y á donde acuderén muchos mas desde el momento en que se ecuentre un especifico seguro contra la cruel enfermendad tropical que arrebeta á una huesa prematura á tantos europeos, asi nacionales como estrangeros.

ANDRES GRAUPERA.

LITERATURE.

1. *Wirkungen des Schlangengiftes,* zum ärztlichen Gebrauche vergleichend zusammengestellt, durch *Constantin Hering,* Allentown, Pa.

2. *Pathogénesies Brésilienne* contenant trente-six experiences pures, par B. Mure. Paris, a l'Institute Homéopathique. Rue de la Harpe, No. 93.

3. *Mure's Materia Medica, or Provings of the principal animal and vegetable Poisons in the Brazilian Empire,* translated from the French by C. J. Hempel, M.D., Article Crotalus Cascarella. New-York, Wm. Radde, 1854. Of this *Crotalus,* Dr. B. Mure says: "It is my belief, that it affects the organism longer and more thoroughly than *Lachesis* and will effect many cures, which had to remain incomplete under the use of *Lachesis.*

4. Quarterly Summary of the Transactions of the college of Physicians of Philadelphia, from August to October inclusive, 1853.

5. Medical Examiner, 1853. Philadelphia.

6. Epidemic Yellow Fever and its Homœopathic Treatment. By William Holcombe, M.D., Natchez, Miss. 1853.

7. Letter to the Editor of the New Orleans Picayune on the Contagiousness of the Disease, from Elgin, S. C.

8. Histoire de l'inoculation preservative de la fièvre jaune, pratiquie par ordre de gouvernement Espagnol á l'Hôpital Militaire de la Havane. Redigèe par *Nicolas B. L. Manzini* (Dr. Forli, Etats Romains), Docteur en Médicine de la faculté de Paris, membre titulaire de la société médicale d'emulation de Paris, Médicin de l'association de bienfaisance française de la Havane. Paris: J. B. Ballière et fils, libraires de l'academie impériale de medicine, rue Hautefeuille, 19. 1860.

9. Smithsonian Contributions to Knowledge. Researches upon the venom of the Rattlesnake, by *S. Weir Mitchell, M.D.,* Lecturer on Physiology.

THE NATURE OF CROTALUS-HORRIDUS.

To illustrate the nature of this poison in its connection with yellow fever, we will detail the chief data of Dr. Mitchell's most interesting experiments and observations:

Fifteen drops of venom was the largest quantity Dr. M. saw ejected from the mouth of the snake, by natural process.

After the first ejection had taken place, the snakes rarely throw out more than from two to four drops.

The color of the venom varied from a *pale emerald green* to *orange* and *straw* color. When the poison had remained long in the gland, it was deeper in hue than when its ejection followed rapidly upon its formation. In eight observations on record the venom reddened litmus paper more or less distinctly. It was uniformly acid, and this reaction was common to all specimens of the poison, whether moist or dry, dark-colored or pale in tint. The reaction of the mucous membrane of the mouth was almost as consistently alkaline as that of the venom was acid. It was found that litmus, reddened by the venom, became blue again when left in the serpent's jaws; but although the acid was neutralized, the poisonous properties of the fluid remained unaltered.

According to Mitchell the venom of the rattlesnake is composed of

1. An albuminoid body. *Crotaline* not coagulable by heat of 212° Fahrenheit.

2. An albuminoid compound, coagulable at 212°.

3. A coloring matter and an undetermined substance; both soluble in alcohol.

4. A trace of fatty matter.

5. Salts, chlorides, and phosphates.

In the numerous experiments made by the author, where the *exhausted venom gland* was mixed with water and introduced into the wounds of various animals, it was ascertained that

ix

the pigeons all escaped, except one; that the rabbit was also unhurt; but the reed birds all died.

The reed bird is remarkably susceptible to Crotalus venom, and will frequently die from a quantity of poison so minute, that it would be hard to conceive of its power to destroy life, had not the experiment actually been made. Thus half a drop will often kill a reed bird in a minute or two, and one-eighth of a drop will prove fatal after a lapse of from two to eight hours; so that it is probable that even a smaller quantity would be sufficient to destroy life.

The secretion in Crotalus from the gland is *constantly acid*, and in the viper *neutral*, while the saliva of the parotid, in all animals yet examined, is unchangeably *alkaline*.

Saliva is a secretion of rapid formation, and appropriated to specific mechanical and chemical purposes within the economy; —the venom fluid is slowly elaborated; slowly reproduced when lost, and destined to no end *within* the body which produces it.

Its singular nature as a ferment; poisonous to other animals as well as to its owner, constitutes a distinction which forbids the physiologist to regard it, as, in any true sense, a salivary secretion, or its forming organ, as a salivary gland. Extensive experiments with chemical reagents, as well as with extremes of heat and cold, have unfolded the singular energy of this poison, and the almost inconceivable tenacity with which its powers are preserved.

The dried venom retained its potency after two years of climatic changes; the fresh poison, although prone to partial decomposition, would remain active after a sojourn of several weeks in an atmosphere of 65° to 70° Fahrenheit.

Mixing the venom with water, and freezing it, and keeping it for half an hour at 4 degrees above zero, did not in the least diminish its power; nor did a temperature of 212° F. destroy its vitality.

In eight experiments Dr. M. has shown that,

1. The coagulum produced by heat is always innocent.

2. The supernatant fluid is uniformly poisonous. The cases died with the usual rapidity.—A fact which leads us to infer that the venom loses no power by being heated. The animals

which perished from the injection of the *boiled venom* exhibited very trifling local evidences of the action of the poison. Dr. M. is unable to offer any plausible explanation of this curious deficiency. (Were he a believer in the dynamic origin of disease and action of remedies, he would be better able to comprehend this phenomenon.)

The mingling of the venom with Alcohol, Sulphuric-acid, Muriatic-ac., Ammonia, Chlorine-water, Iodine, Soda and Potassa, in a diluted or undiluted state, did not destroy the virulence of the venom.

When venom was mingled with certain of these agents, such as Iodine in solution, Tannic-acid, &c., the *constitutional symptoms declared themselves* as usual in the pigeons employed; but the local phenomena were more or less wanting.

The Crotalus venom has the power of preventing the germination of canary and mignionette seeds.

"On several occasions," I quote the words of Dr. M., "I had noticed the production of fungi in moist venom, long kept upon my table, in an atmosphere of from 64° to 70° F."

"I have also observed in other specimens long kept, and somewhat diluted, that after seven to ten days, the poison acquired an odor of a peculiar and very disgusting character. The production of this animalized and indescribable stench, was accompanied by the appearance of vibriones, and, a few days later, of rotiferal and other minute forms of animalcular life. The question was, what power yet remained in the venom which had become the nidus of so much active vitality. I tested it on animals, and still found it actively poisonous."

From the same work we gather the following interesting data—particularly such phenomena as may have reference to Yellow or Bilious Fevers.

"Both pigeons were enfeebled by the poison, and seemed disposed to sleep. One of them sunk slowly, lower and lower, until its head touched the table, when it rolled on its side.

In ten minutes, a pigeon, after it was struck on the back by a small snake, fell into the *usual stupor*, with jerking, abrupt respiration, &c. The bird became gradually weaker and weaker, and died without convulsions, at the close of an hour and a half. The pupils gradually contracted before death, and suddenly dilated afterwards.

The tissues, for an inch or more around the wound, were soaked with extravasated blood, which had even passed through between the ribs, so as to stain the *tissues* behind the intestines.

The heart was large and full of perfectly fluid blood.

"My chief reason for recording at length these cases," continues Dr. Mitchell, "is to show the *great increase in the internal lesions which occurs, when the venom is long in killing the animal.*"

Among these changes it was found, as a general rule, that the blood was most affected, and least coagulable, the longer death was delayed.

In two cases the dogs passed *clay-colored* stools.

So far as a fatal result is concerned, it seems to be indifferent, whether the bite takes place about the head and neck, or in the limbs.

This last observation is of great interest owing to the fact, that the dog, a small terrier, survived very serious visceral lesions, and lived during two days, with his blood in a condition of complete diffluence.

Twenty hours from the time of the poisoning, the dog was found lying on his left side, having passed shiny and bloody stools in abundance. At intervals he seemed to suffer much from tenesmus, but was so weak, that he stood up with difficulty. *His gums were bleeding, a symptom I had seen before, and his eyes were deeply injected.* (The most characteristic symptom of Yellow Fever, according to Manzini.)

Twenty-seven hours and a half after the time he was bitten, his hind legs were twitching and the dysentery continued. No clot was found in the blood. This case is doubly important because it shows how long the poisoning must continue before the blood becomes diffluent.

Dr. Mitchell continues :

"The study of the envenomed blood has thus far taught us:

1st. That in animals which survive the poisoning for a time, the blood is so altered as to render the fibrin incoagulable.

2d. Experiments in and out of the body have given proof,

that this change is gradual, and that the absence of coagulation is not due to checked formation of fibrin, but to alterations produced by the action of the venom in that fibrin which already exists in the circulating blood.

3d. The influence thus exerted is of a putrefactive nature, and imitates, *in a few hours*, the ordinary work of days of change. It is probably even more rapid within the body, on account of the higher temperature of the economy.

4th. The altered blood retains its power to absorb gases, and thus to change its own color.

5th. The blood corpuscles are unaffected in acute poisoning by Crotalus venom, and are rarely and doubtfully altered in the most prolonged cases which result fatally.

6th. The contents of the blood globules of the guinea pig can be made to crystallize, as is usual after other modes of death.

Among the most constant and curious lesions in the cases of *secondary poisoning are the ecchymosis, which are found on and in the viscera of the chest and belly, most frequently affecting the intestinal canal.* They may and do occur in any cavity and on any organ. These spots contain blood, whose globules are more or less deformed, but still of dimensions not less that usual. * * * *

Owing to the changes of the blood, or the tissues, or both, extravasations are met with in the lungs, brain, kidneys, serous membranes, intestines and heart. As a result we may have functional derangement grafted on the main stem of the malady and the accompaniments of bloody serum in the affected cavities, bloody mucus in the intestinal canal, and bloody urine in the bladder."

From the preceding experiments Dr. Mitchell naturally arrives at the conclusion: "That the venom of Crotalus, like that of other snakes is *a septic, or putrefacient poison of astounding energy;* a view long held by toxicologists.

The rapid decomposition of the blood, and of the tissues locally acted upon by the venom, leaves no doubt upon the matter, and makes it apparent that an incipient putrefaction of this nature may so affect the blood as to destroy its power to clot, and perhaps, also, to nourish the tissues through which it is urged."

The alterations thus brought about are, probably, the results of a continued fermentative change, which, begun by a small amount of poison, is gradually made to involve in fatal change, the whole mass of the circulating fluids. *Like all fermentations, however, the rapidity depends upon temperature, and on the amount of the primary ferment.*

In one instance, a dog, struck by eight snakes died in eighteen minutes, and exhibited uncoagulable blood.

I am aware of no other case of loss of uncoagulable blood so rapid.

It was rendered thus by the number of localities from which the ferment attacked the system.

On the other hand, the frog, a small animal, receives the same dose of venom as would have entered the tissues of a larger animal; yet it resists the poison most remarkably, by virtue of its powers as a cold-blooded creature, existing at the temperature of the atmosphere itself.

The cause of death in *chronic or secondary poisoning,* may, with propriety, then be referred to the incipient putrefactive changes, which affect the blood, as well as to the continued influence of the agencies, which first act to depress the heart's action, and destroy nerve function.

Summing up what we have learnt of the *acute forms of poisoning,* we may feel justified, according to Dr. Mitchell, in concluding:

1st. That the heart becomes enfeebled shortly after the bite. This is due to *direct influence of the venom on this organ,* and not to the *precedent* loss of the *respiratory function.* Notwithstanding the diminution of the cardial power, the heart is usually in motion after the lungs cease to act, and its tissues remain, for a time, locally irritable. The paralysis of the heart is, therefore, not so complete as it is under the influence of upas or corroval.

2d. That, in warm-blooded animals, artificial respiration lengthens the life of the heart, but does not sustain it so long as where the animal has died by woorara or decapitation.

3d. That in frogs the heart-acts continue after respiration has ceased, and sometimes survive until the sensory nerves and the nerve-centres are dead; the motor nerves alone remaining irritable.

4th. That in warm-blooded animals respiration ceases, owing to paralysis of the nerve-centres.

5th. That the *sensory nerves,* and the *centres* of *nerve power,* in the *medulla spinalis* and the *medulla oblongata, lose their vitality before the efferent or motor nerves become affected.*

6th. That the muscular system retains its irritability in the cold-blooded animals, acutely poisoned, for a considerable time after death.

7th. That the first effect of the venom being to depress the vital energy of the heart and nerve centres, a resort to stimulants is clearly indicated, as the only rational mode of early constitutional treatment.

Dr. *S. Weir Mitchell* concludes this chapter on the action of the venom on the tissues and fluids, from which we have made such copious extracts with the following remarkable sentences:

ANALOGY BETWEEN CROTALUS POISONING AND THE SYMPTOMS OF CERTAIN DISEASES.

I am unwilling to leave this unsatisfactory, but necessary part of my task, without calling attention to the singular likeness between the symptoms and lesions of Crotalus poisoning and those of certain maladies, such as Yellow Fever.* If for a moment we lose sight of the local injection, and regard only the symptoms which follow, and the tissue changes which ensue, the resemblance becomes still more striking.

In both diseases—for such they are—we have a class of cases in which death seems to occur suddenly, and inexplicably, as though caused by an overwhelming dose of the poison. In both diseases these cases are marked by symptoms of profound prostration, and in both the post-mortem revelations fail to explain the death. I have spoken, as an example, of Yellow Fever, but similar instances are not wanting in Cholera, Typhoid and Typhus fevers, and in Scarlatina."

---

* This analogy has been noted by *S. L. Mitchell,* by Magendie, and by Gaspard, who has also called attention to the resemblance between ordinary putrefactive poisoning, such as arises from injection into the blood of decayed animal substances, and the poisoning by venom.

"A second class of cases, both of Crotalus poisoning, and of Yellow Fever, survive the first shock of the malady, and then begin to exhibit the train of symptoms, which terminates in more or less complete degradation of the character of the blood, varying remarkably among themselves, exhibiting, as it were, preferences for this, or that organ; all these maladies agree in the destruction of the fibrin of the blood, which these fatal cases frequently exhibit. In Yellow Fever, the likeness to the venom poisoning is most distinctly preserved, as we trace the symptoms of both diseases to the point where the diffluent blood leaks out into the mucous and serous cavities. The yellowness which characterizes many Yellow Fever cases, I do not find described as a current symptom of the venom malady, but it is often mentioned as one of the accompaniments of the period of recovery from the bite.* It is indeed most probable, that if small and repeated doses of venom were introduced, at intervals, into the body of an animal, a disease might be produced even more nearly resembling the malady in question. In the parallel thus drawn, I have given the broad outlines of resemblance; nor was it to be expected that the minor details would be alike. From a general and philosophic point of view, this similarity is sufficiently striking to make me hope, that the complete control of one such septic poison for experimental use, may enable us, in future, to throw new light on those septic poisons of disease, of whose composition we know nothing of, and whose very means of entering the body they destroy, is as yet a mystery.

PHILADELPHIA, 1867.

---

* Jaundice, occasionally observed in France, as an early symptom of viper-bite, has been usually regarded as the Jaundice of fear; a cause which certainly cannot be invoked to account for the icterus, seen in the last stages of the malady, caused by the venom.

THE EFFICACY OF CROTALUS HORRIDUS

IN

Yellow and Malignant, Bilious and Remittent Fevers.

CHAPTER I.

YELLOW FEVER IN PHILADELPHIA DURING THE SUMMER
AND AUTUMN OF 1853.

On the 25th of June, 1853, the bark *Mandarin* sailed from Cienfuegos, Cuba, for Philadelphia, all in good health, with a cargo of sugar, molasses, and segars. Her crew consisted of twelve men.

On arriving at the Lazaretto, July 12th, after a voyage of seventeen days, she was visited by the officers of the station; and, on oath, the captain reported cases of small-pox and fever when he left, and that he had lost two of his crew on the passage with fever. The statement of the Lazaretto physician was: "that the crew, numbering ten souls, were examined, and reported to be in good health; notwithstanding this it was considered prudent that the bark should be detained until thoroughly ventilated, cleansed, and fumigated; the bedding and clothing of the deceased sailors were destroyed, the vessel was whitewashed and fumigated in every part with chloride of lime, the bedding of the crew aired, and their clothing washed; she was detained an entire day, and, before being allowed to proceed to Philadelphia, all on board were separately and minutely examined. All hands were on duty, and apparently free from disease.

There was no development of disease of a malignant type in the vicinity where this vessel lay, after the strictest inquiry instituted by the port physician. Nor had any of her sailors and laborers, employed in removing the cargo, been sick. But, when the cargo was out of the vessel, a very offensive smell proceeded from her hold; especially whenever her pumps agitated the bilge-water contained under the planks of the flooring, the stench became intolerable.

The first case of suspicious fever was on the 19th of July, the day before which the *Mandarin* left her position on Lombard-street wharf; a young man, whose stand was at South-street wharf, sickened and died. The next case was that of a captain, whose brig lay at Lombard-street wharf, and who slept on board the brig, and took his meals at the Champion House; he took sick on the 20th. The next case was the son of Mr. Koehler, who lived with his father at the Champion House. The next was the keeper of the Red Bank Ferry House, and his wife, in the same vicinity. Up to July 27, there were seventeen cases, of which eleven died. There were only eight of these cases which exhibited black vomit, and they all perished. In the month of August there were twenty-seven additional cases—presenting, in all respects, evidence of yellow fever—twenty-three of which died.

In eleven of the thirty-four a post-mortem was made; in all of which the yellow or ochre-colored liver was detected in whole or in part. In all of them the "coffee-ground" fluid, or melanic blood, was found, either in the stomach or intestines, with other evidence of pernicious form of fever. The mortality was fearful, 80 per cent., or five to one of recoveries. The disease still continued to prevail till the 7th of October, when the last case occurred. During this period, of eighty days, there were one hundred and seventy cases. They included every variety of the disease, or those recognized in the nomenclature of yellow, malignant, malignant remittent, pernicious, malignant bilious, and typhus-icterodes fevers. One hundred and forty-seven of these cases may be distinctly traced to the immediate vicinity of the infected district, making South-street wharf the centre.

It was here the bark *Mandarin* landed, which brought the fever. Of the remainder, it is uncertain where the fever was contracted. The ratio of mortality was very large—out of 170 cases there were 128 deaths, equal to 75 per cent.

This mortality must be ascribed to the virulence of the miasmatic poison, for which the allopathic treatment hitherto pursued proved entirely inadequate. It must not, however, be overlooked that there have been other cases of fever in the infected locality, assuming a less malignant form, which were not reported to the

Board of Health. If these had been included in the above estimate they would have diminished the ratio of mortality. Among all the cases of malignant fever that happened in 1853, in Philadelphia, of which we have any record, there is not a single instance of its occurrence among the colored population. This fact is in accordance with a generally received observation that the African race is much less susceptible to malarious influences than others. The late Dr. Campos, of Norfolk, Va., averred that very fat people got over it very well; while Dr. Antonio Leon Bilisoly, of the same place, asserted the contrary.

CHAPTER II.

CONTAGIOUS OR NON-CONTAGIOUS?

THE non-contagiousness of the disease has been again maintained in the epidemic of 1853, and it is averred that, *although many of the cases contracted by a visit to the infected district were treated far beyond its limits, in different parts of the city, in no one instance was the disease communicated from one person to another.* In the Pennsylvania Hospital, twenty-four cases were treated, and in wards surrounded by those who were sick and convalescent from other diseases, and where there was continual intercourse with the patients, still not an individual in the house was attacked with the fever. The like immunity was observed in the Blockley

Hospital, where, had the disease possessed contagious qualities, it would very likely have spread among the inmates.

Such is the specious reasoning of the non-contagionists, who, at first sight, would seem to have all the facts and reasoning in their favor. But these facts rather prove too much. It is not denied that, at the wharf, or where-ever the disease was in a concentrated form, many persons were affected by it, either by clothes or by contact.

Let us review the facts of some former epidemics. In the year 1748, Dr. Lining, an eminent physician of Charleston, S. C., gives a minute account of the yellow fever of that year, and states that the disease had been epidemic during several previous years in that town, and that, in every instance, " it was easily traced to some person who had lately arrived from the West India Islands, where it was epidemical." Dr. Chisholm, a surgeon to the British forces in the West Indies, states that this epidemic (1793) was brought by a ship to Granada, one of the Windward Islands ; that from this island, to use his words, " it spread to the other islands—to Jamaica, St. Domingo, and also to Philadelphia—by means of vessels on board which the infection was retained by the clothes, more especially the woolen jackets of the sailors." He also further states " that the disease appeared in several distinct and distant parts of the island, whither the infection was carried by persons who had imprudently visited the infected houses in the town."

The clothing of a victim to yellow fever in the West

Indies was sent on and retained for a long time boxed up tightly at the North, and, when finally opened, caused the death, by yellow fever, of the person who took possession of the clothing. This happened in the interior of New-Jersey (*New-Orleans Picayune*, 1854). We must also here refer to the case of the family dwelling upon the hills, back of Fort Adams, who had no communication with the river, and among whom the disease suddenly broke out in 1853, and which was referred to by the advocates of non-contagion. Upon investigation, it turns out that this family had received a sack of Rio coffee and a bale of goods from New-Orleans during the height of the epidemic there. Neither is there any doubt that every case of the disease, not readily accounted for by contagion, would be found traceable to contact with goods or groceries received from cities or towns infected with the disease. In some plantations the disease was introduced and prevailed epidemically among the Negroes from contact with the rope or bagging received from New-Orleans.

Of this same epidemic, of 1853, which, in Philadelphia, spread only to a limited extent, Dr. Holcombe, of Natchez, furnishes the following facts with regard to that locality: " The first cases appeared in families, some member or members of which had come from New-Orleans within a few weeks. The houses were not under the hill, along the river, nor in the suburbs, nor in filthy, ill-ventilated, damp, and otherwise noxious places, where, if at all, the disease might be supposed to originate. They were pleasantly situated in the central parts of the city, and the tenants all in comfortable circum-

stances. There were three centres of emanation, whence
the disease appeared to spread in every direction, not
reaching the suburbs until after the lapse of several
weeks. Many of the inhabitants, who fled to the country, carried the disease with them. One gentleman
sickened on the road, and stopped at the house of a
friend twelve miles from town, where he died of yellow
fever. One of the family speedily exhibited the same
disease, and died ; another fled into an adjoining county,
where he also sickened, and communicated the disease
to those around him." In several cases which came under Dr. Holcombe's observation, the families in the
country were carefully isolated, with the exception of
one messenger, who was permitted to visit the town on
necessary business, and uniformly the messenger was
the one first attacked.

From all these facts, which are no doubt well authen-
ticated, we are led to conclude that the yellow fever shows
itself in its deadliest form only when concentrated, as on
board of a ship, particularly in woollen clothing, and
can thus be propagated *ad libitum*. But when diluted,
by being spread over a large part of the town to the
Pennsylvania Hospital and Blockley Almshouse, its
virulence is exhausted, and the disease is only propagated
in a milder form. The disease is modified by being
communicated from one person to another ; and some
are only sick for a few days, or have but a few of its
symptoms, so that no one would admit this to be the
terrible disease, yellow fever, although produced by the
same potent cause. Whilst attending my slighter cases
of yellow fever, I was invariably affected by a few cha-

racteristic symptoms of the disease, which, however, soon passed away. One case of this kind, subsequently observed, was very striking. During the violent epidemic of 1856, Mr. ——, went to Norfolk to nurse the sick. After his return home he was attacked by the disease, and died under allopathic treatment. His daughter, Mrs. S., my patient, merely saw the corpse, and was, in a few days afterwards, attacked by some symptoms very characteristic of yellow fever. I told her husband that if I did not know that there was no disease of the kind in the city, I would suppose it was a slight attack of yellow fever. At the time I was not aware of her father having died of that disease, and her having visited the corpse. But, still further, his wife, having nursed him during his illness, afterwards went into the country, and was there seized with violent pains in her head, with bilious vomiting, &c. She soon recovered. These persons were not severely affected by the yellow fever, but their symptoms were evidently produced by the same miasmatic virus. Is this strange? Is not the whole theory of homœopathy based upon this fact? Do not all our remedies act, in a diluted form, much milder than when concentrated? Do we not, on the other hand, know that this action is very much influenced or modified by what we call the peculiar susceptibility of the patient or individual to the particular poison? We may, I think, lay down two axioms as nearly correct: 1. That yellow fever will only show its deadliest effect when in its most concentrated form ; 2. That there must be a peculiar susceptibility of the individual to this particular poison at the time of his exposure, in order to show its most penetrating effect.

This view of the question of contagion and non-contagion holds good with all epidemics. Cholera, *e. g.*, furnishes its greatest number of victims with those first attacked, whilst, during the progress of the disease, the cases are constantly getting milder. In the case of small-pox a similar law prevails.

CHAPTER III.

ANALYSIS OF THE PATHOGNOMONIC SYMPTOMS OF THE YELLOW FEVER (1853) IN TEN CASES, AS FURNISHED BY DR. GILBERT, THE PORT PHYSICIAN.

FEVER, without remission, until the end of the third day, then prostration without reaction, in every case.

Sallow skin and eye, bronzed color of skin, sallowness of conjunctiva, are mentioned in *four* cases; yellow skin in *two* cases.

In *three* cases there was black vomiting.

Hæmorrhage from mucous surfaces, *two* cases.

Excruciating pain in the loins in *three* cases. In addition to this, in *one* case, pain in the head and limbs.

In those that recovered there was no yellow or bronzed skin; no black vomit; but in two there was headache and nausea.

2

ANALYSIS OF THE SYMPTOMS OF THIRTY-FOUR ADDITIONAL CASES, TWENTY-SEVEN OF WHICH WERE REPORTED BY DR. JEWELL, AND NINE FROM THE PRIVATE PRACTICE OF DR. STOKES, OF PHILADELPHIA.

Some symptoms may have been more frequent, but, as they were not found in the record, I could, of course, not mention them. I have been limited to the often imperfect delineation, partly because, the physicians attending neglected to make careful notes, and, partly, they were only called in at the more advanced stage of the disease, and thus received an imperfect relation of the previous symptoms by the nurses and friends of the family.

The symptoms were, no doubt, also modified by the allopathic treatment; although I have never seen any disease that is less modified by medical treatment than this fever, unless the remedy is absolutely specific. In twenty-six of the forty-four cases there occurred the peculiar dark-colored "coffee-ground" ejection from the stomach, known as the black vomit. This substance, when placed within the field of the microscope, exhibited the true blood-corpuscles, denoting its sanguineous character.

HEAD.

Severe pain is mentioned in *eighteen* cases; in one case there was more headache than any other symptom the second day, less pain in the head and limbs after taking Calomel, Rhubarb, Nitre, and Ipecacuanha. In *one* case, the disease commenced with excessive pain over the right eye and temple at night.

Great pain in back of head in *two* cases ; and in *one* case back of neck also.

EARS.

Considerable deafness in *one* case, and slight in *two* cases. (Two drachms of Quinine were taken in two of them, and also large doses of Ipecac., Quinine, and Calomel in one of them.)

EYES.

Eyes injected is mentioned in *thirteen* cases ; slightly in *four* cases. Conjunctiva red and slightly tinged with brown, the second day, *one* case. Eyes red and fiery, *three* cases. Eyes red and fiery, and yellow, *one* case. Eyes purulent, *one* case (after taking Calomel, five grains, every two hours for a day).

NOSE.

Hæmorrhage frequent from the nose during the third and fourth day, in *six* cases.

FACE.

Face dark, suffused, or flushed, is mentioned in *three* cases ; the second day, with an expression of greatest anxiety, in *one* case.

Purplish tint on face and upper extremities (after taking five grains of Calomel every two hours).

Less suffusion of countenance the fourth day, *one* case.

Suffusion of countenance, giving the tipsy look so common in this disease, second day, *one* case. (Is this the reason why alcoholic drinks are so useful in this disease as curatives ?)

TONGUE.

Tongue perfectly natural in *two* cases ; or to the touch in *two* cases. Tongue moist in *two* cases; with paste-like centre *two* cases; with pale red edges *two* cases; tongue bright red, third day, *one* case ; red at the tip and edges, fifth day, *one* case; the same patient had the tongue dry and the teeth covered with black sordes on the sixth day. Tongue coated white in *eight* cases, with bright-red edges in *five* cases. Tongue scarlet-red, first day, *one* case. Tongue coated and dry, presenting a brownish appearance, much worse on second day, *one* case. Tongue furred and soft in *three* cases. Tongue less moist, deeper red, second day, in *two* cases. Tongue dry, parched, red like raw beef, on the second day; red at the edges, dark in centre and base, on the third and fourth day, in *one* case. Tongue white in centre, with pale-red edges, became fiery red on the second day, in *one* case.

EPIGASTRIUM.

Intense epigastric uneasiness, with great tenderness on pressure, in *twelve* cases.

Great distress over epigastric region, oppression about the heart, and nausea, with fever, continuing five days, when the fever abated. From that time to the period of death—fourteen days—the above symptoms continued unabated until she died, one case.

Pain in the epigastrium, increased by pressure, the second day, in *three* cases.

Tenderness all over the abdomen in a woman of seventy years of age. Tenderness in the epigastrium on second day (after large doses of Ipecac. and Quinine), oppression over sternum and anterior portion of thorax, as if a very heavy weight were laid there, *one* case.

Intense *thirst* on the afternoon of the second day in *two* cases.

Intense thirst on the first day of the disease in *six* cases. Some *nausea* is mentioned in *one* case on the first day, and in *one* on the fourth day.

Constant *nausea* on the second day in *three* cases. (One of these patients, after taking Calomel and Rhubarb, had the next day no nausea, nor tenderness of the epigastrium.)

Nausea and *vomiting* on the first day, *one* case.

Nausea on the first day, but not on the second (after Ipecac. and Quinine).

Vomiting of food, then froth, but no bile, in *one* case.

Stomach exceedingly irritable in *two* cases, ejecting everything, even ice-water, *one* case.

Vomiting of a watery fluid in *two* cases.

Vomiting of glairy mucus in *one* case.

Continual vomiting in *two* cases; the vomiting in one case, which recovered, occurred at intervals.

Black vomit, or like coffee-grounds, or lees of porter, in *twenty-six* out of the *forty-four* cases.

Vomiting of grayish fluid, mixed with blood, on the second day of the disease, in *one* case.

Bowels costive in *four* cases; on the first day is mentioned in *two* cases.

Bowels loose, moved four times a day, *one* case (after taking a drachm of Magnesia.

Bowels moved twice, first and second days, *one* case.

Bilious evacuations (after four grains of Calomel and one-quarter grain of Opium). Evacuations of dark color and tar-like consistence (also after repeated doses of Calomel), *one* case.

Several copious stools, of green color, on the second day, *one* case.

Evacuations of orange-yellow color on the fourth day in one who recovered.

URINE.

Complete suppression of urine on the first day, but the same patient passed some water on the second day.

Suppression of urine on the fourth day (in one who died afterwards).

Urine scanty first day in *one* who died.

Respiration hurried the second day is mentioned in *one* case.

BACK.

Back of neck, intense pain.

Lumbar region or back, severe pain in *fourteen* cases.

EXTREMITIES.

Pain or cramps in the limbs in *ten* cases; in *three* the calf of the legs is mentioned; excessive pain in the legs on being roused up at night in *two* cases.

Pain in fingers or toe-joints in *one* case.

Extremities cool, *one* case.

PULSE.

Pulse, as being full hard and frequent, is mentioned in *two* cases on the second day; as being feeble in another case; then, again, in one who recovered, the pulse was at first sinking, but became afterwards full and tense.

The frequency of the pulse varied in almost every patient.

In one who recovered it was 78; then again pulse varying from 80 to 100 in *one* case.

Pulse 80, *two* cases (after five grains of Quinine and a large dose of Ipecac.)

Pulse varying from 86 to 90; at first full, afterwards feeble and small.

Pulse 82, regular, and of ordinary fullness, first day.

Pulse 86, second day.

Pulse 98, first day, of moderate strength and fullness; second day more feeble. Recovered.

Pulse 100 in *two* cases. First day full and tense; on the second day 120, full and tense.

Pulse 100; harder and fuller on the third day.

Pulse 104, feeble and compressible. Same person, second day:

Pulse 120, weak and compressible.

Pulse 110, *one* case.

Pulse 115, full, tense.

Pulse 120, strong and active first day in two cases; 114 second day.

Pulse 129 at first; the third day 106, and on the fourth day 92.

Pulse 130 throughout in *one* case.

FEVER.

Chills, followed by *fever*, in *five* cases.

Chills, followed by severe fever, in *four* cases.

Chills, followed by fever, *two* cases the first day.

Chilly first and second day, *one* case.

Very little fever in *one* case.

Violent fever, in a woman of seventy, first day.

High fever for two days, *one* case.

High fever, with great thirst and drowsiness, one case.

Some chilliness, cold extremities, one case.

Severe chills, *one* case.

Burning internally, one case.

Delirium on the third day in *two* cases.

Delirium slight in *three* cases on second day.

Muttering delirium, *one* case.

Delirium increasing in second stage, *one* case.

Depression of spirits, one case.

SKIN.

Body covered with a petechial eruption, *one* case.

Red spots over the extremities, *one* case.

Skin, from the commencement of the attack, was of a yellow hue in *four* cases.

Skin began to be yellow on the second day, *one* case.

General yellow hue of skin and conjunctiva in *four* cases.

The blister which had been applied over the epigastrium, on being cut, stained his linen a yellow hue.

Yellowness made its appearance on the third day of sickness (in *one* who died).

Skin hot and dry in *four* cases, but not yellow.

Skin burning and dry in *one* case.

Heat of skin less marked on second day, and still less on third, *one* case.

Heat of skin considerable on second day, *one* case.

Skin somewhat moist on second day, *one* case.

GENERAL SYMPTOMS.

Great *debility* in *three* cases.

Such prostration of strength at the beginning of the disease that he was with difficulty enabled to reach his residence, only two squares distant, and from which he had walked with ease only one hour and a half before.

Lassitude, *one* case.

Great prostration first and second day, *one* case.

At the very commencement of the disease great prostration, *one* case.

General soreness, *one* case.

Stupor is mentioned in *one* case.

Less stupid the second day, in the afternoon; stupor increased the third day, one case.

SLEEP.

Considerable drowsiness.

Restlessness and drowsiness, with coma, in *two* cases. (One of these patients had fallen from a height a week before.)

Restlessness at night with delirium, second night, hard to rouse, one case.

Patient sleeps almost continuously.

Little sleep during the second night of the disease, one case.

SYMPTOMS OCCURRING DURING THE LAST STAGE OF THE
DISEASE, OR BEFORE DEATH.

Mind muddy, but answered correctly when questioned.

Mind clear one day before death, in *two* cases.

Difficult to rouse; intellect dull one day before death.

Headache one day before death mentioned in *one* case.

The *eye* at this stage assumes a peculiar pinkish hue in *five* cases.

Before death the eye became jaundiced, and the skin bronzed in appearance, in *two* cases.

Five hours before death the eyes are of a delicate pink color, slightly streaked with yellow, *one* case.

Eyes lustreless, conjunctiva injected, one day before death.

Epistaxis of dark blood in the morning, and returning in the evening, with rapid prostration, one case.

Tongue remains clean, *one* case.

Tongue large and soft, white in middle, with red edges and tip, *one* case.

Tongue thickly coated white on second day, the patient dying in forty-eight hours.

One day before death, tongue intensely red, dry, and protruded with difficulty, *one* case.

Tongue red at tip and edges, with brown dry centre; sordes on the teeth one day before death, *one* case.

Expectoration of a little blood before death.

Black vomit in twenty-six cases out of the forty-four.

Rejected everything taken into the stomach, resisting all stimulants, gulping up everything by the mouthful, in *two* cases.

Very tender over the *epigastrium* and the right iliac fossa, one case.

Extreme tenderness of the *epigastrium* one day before death in *three* cases.

When in articulo-mortis, the *evacuations* from his bowels were liquid, and of a darker color than the matter vomited, in *three* cases.

Dark fluid discharges, tinged with blood, on the third day, *one* case.

Several black and bloody stools during the night, one case.

Involuntary black and watery discharges, one case.

Intense *thirst* fifth day, *one* case.

Suppression of *urine* one day before death.

Pulse 108, soft and regular.

Pulse more feeble, *two* cases.

Pulseless; sinking rapidly on the second day, *one* case.

Pulseless on the fifth day, without sense or motion: died without convulsion, *one* case.

Pulse about 80, feeble, and very compressible, one day before death, *one* case.

GENERAL SYMPTOMS.

Convulsions before death in *two* cases.

Continual sighing and tossing in bed, *one* case.

Muscular tremors, one case.

Extremities cold one day before death.

Great *prostration* on the fifth day in two cases; in *one* case on the third, and *another* on the fourth day.

Patient lies motionless on the seventh day, one day before death, *one* case.

Sinking on the sixth, *one* case.

Three died on the sixth day, 3, P. M.; *one* on the eighth, and *two* on the fifth day. *One* died three hours after admission into the St. Joseph's Hospital; *one* died in fourteen days, and *one* in three days and a half; *two* in forty-eight hours.

Four deaths occurred on the fourth day, and *three* on the second day; *one* on the third, and one on the thirteenth day. *One* case was cured in seven days, which, according to Dr. Gilbert, the port physician, seems not to have been genuine yellow fever.

One patient, who died on the eighth day of his disease, said, not long before his death, that he felt "*very well, as if he were going to the other world.*" In this case the symptoms have not been detailed after the second day, as large doses of Quinine and Calomel modified them to such a degree that they would be of very little account.

SKIN.

Skin cold and system collapsed, *one* case.

Skin cold and clammy; numerous small spots, injected, of a deep red color, made their appearance upon the neck, breast, and arms, as it were in clusters.

The eye and skin before death were slightly tinged of a yellow hue.

Skin cool and of a pale lemon color one day before death, *one* case.

One day before death increase of sallowness, extending to abdomen, *one* case.

Before death skin bronzed appearance, *one* case.

One day before death skin became very yellow in *three* cases, accompanied with the greatest sensibility to the slightest touch, in *one* case.

Five hours before death the yellow skin was most conspicuous on the breast and neck, *one* case.

On the second day the skin of the person who died in forty-eight hours became yellow universally, increasing in intensity toward the evening of the same day. Thirty hours after death the body became quite black.

Skin very yellow after death, *one* case.

Six hours after death skin is very yellow; vibices on extremities very dark in color, in a woman of seventy.

Five hours after death skin deep yellow, mottled with purple down the back; lower extremities less yellow, *one* case.

Dark-yellowish tint, very marked in about twelve hours after death, although but little yellowness had been observed *during life, one* case.

Of the forty-four cases thirty-four died.

The mean duration of the disease in those who died was *four* days.

The *black vomit*, when placed within the field of the microscope, exhibited the true blood-corpuscles.

In eleven of the thirty-four deaths a post-mortem was made, in all of which the yellow or ochre-colored liver was detected, in whole or in part.

In all of them the "coffee-ground" fluid, or melanic blood, was found, either in the stomach or intestines, with other evidences of a pernicious form of fever.

CHAPTER IV.

ALLOPATHIC TREATMENT.

On reviewing the treatment of the different writers we are not surprised that thirty-four died out of forty-four cases—a mortality equal to eighty per cent.

No indications are furnished by these writers of any individual application of a particular remedy. After the enumeration of a few of the most prominent symptoms, the author says: "Ordered Calomel, ten grains every two hours, and then Quinine, ten grains." The next day these remedies are changed, without giving any reason. It is *just* like the mariner steering without compass or rudder in the wide ocean.

Calomel, Epsom-salts, with Quinine, aggravated one case which was subsequently benefitted by Chlorate of Potash in solution.

Removal from the infected district was one of the best means of preventing a fatal issue.

In one case, that of a nursing mother, the return of the milk was the most favorable sign.

Dr. Jewell, the reporter of the cases to the Medical Society of Philadelphia, speaks of the treatment pursued as follows: "In the first stage of the fever the treatment in general has been by blood-letting from the arm, and by cups to the back and abdomen, emetics mercurial purges, diaphoretics, &c. During the second stage, or as soon as a remission took place—which was generally about the third and fourth day from the attack—Calomel, as a sialogogue, was administered in some cases, in others Quinine, in three or four-grain doses, every one or two hours. In the event of no speedy reaction, Brandy or Wine internally, and local stimulating applications, by blisters and rubefacients, were resorted to.

" Quinine, in full doses, on the first intimation of a remission from fever, appears to have been a favorite remedy. In some cases over seventy grains were administered daily for several days, and, as far as we could learn, without any annoyance to the brain, or other organ, but with advantage. (? !) It will be remembered, however, that the cases at the Blockley Almshouse Hospital were treated without Quinine in any stage of the disease. Calomel, pushed to salivation, was the principal remedy employed."

Such is the model treatment of the best allopathic physicians of Philadelphia in the nineteenth century; and all this with the full knowledge of the superiority of the simple treatment of the Creole nurses in New-Orleans over the usual Calomel treatment, to say nothing of the acknowledged success, in this disease, of the homœopathic physicians at New-Orleans, Charleston, Natchez, and Norfolk.

CHAPTER V.

ALTHOUGH yellow fever did not prevail very extensively or epidemically in Philadelphia during the year 1853, nevertheless the victims which it claimed were not a few, and its ancient character of virulence was fully manifested.

The first case which fell under my notice presented some peculiar features. It was that species which, from the beginning, assumes a typhoid form.

M. W., aged seventeen, having come in contact with a person from the so-called infected district, complained the next day of drowsiness, pain in the bones, sleeplessness, &c., presenting, on the second and third day, the following group of symptoms:

In the middle of the day, from eleven, A. M., to four, P. M., there ensues a febrile paroxysm, with burning heat and redness on the left cheek—the whole face assuming a mahogany color; the mouth is half open, and the patient lays in bed with his eyes shut. On being questioned, he always answers that he has confused sensation in the forehead, as if a tight band was tied over his eyes to the back of the head, with giddiness. Towards evening the fever remits, but he is never entirely free from it.

The skin has a peculiar uniformly hot sensation to the touch. The pulse was from 80 to 90. Bleeding of the nose for several days, sometimes as much as half a pint.

To this he had been formerly subject—the blood coagulating with difficulty. The tongue was dry and parched, black in the centre, the edges slightly moist; tip of tongue very red and dry. Great thirst. One morning also vomiting of bile.

The fifth day pain and swelling of the stomach, with soreness to the touch; in the night slightly delirious. Constipation of the bowels at the commencement, but, during the progress of the disease, he often had diarrhœa. The urine was yellow, cloudy, and he only passed a small quantity. Deafness.

As I had then never seen a case of yellow fever—knowing its character and symptoms only from books and lectures, I called in Dr. Howard, of this city, who had the reputation of being familiar with the disease during his residence in Cuba. He immediately pronounced it to be a genuine case of the disease, and of the typhoid form.

TREATMENT.

Aconit.-nap., 1, and Rhus-tox., 1, repeated every one to two hours, relieved the thirst, the bleeding of the nose, and pain in the stomach; but the other symptoms remained the same.

The patient received consecutively, from September 20 to 21, Aconite and Nux-vomica; September 22, Opium, 1, Bellad., 6; and in the evening of the twenty-third of September, Crotalus Horridus, 7, in water, in alternation with Bellad., 6; finally, up to the first of October, the following remedies: Arsenic, 3, Hippom.-mancinel-

3

la, 7, Lachesis, 6, Merc.-sol., 1, Sulphur, 1, Phosph. and Phosph.-ac., 2, Veratrum, Kreosote, and Quinine.

These remedies were repeated every hour or two hours; for the obstinacy and inveteracy of the disease was so great that, if the remedies were not thus often repeated, the disease would assume an alarming form.

The sopor, dry tongue, fever, &c., were most conspicuously relieved by Kreosote and Phosph.-acid; but the improvement only lasted a day, and the symptoms always returned with the same violence, and I did not consider myself justified in continuing longer their exhibition.

A slight perspiration only was produced during the first day by Aconite, and a profuse one at the crisis, towards the twenty-first day, by *Crotalus Horridus*, 3.* That this crisis was very much aided, if not entirely produced by Crotalus Horridus, in the lower triturations, we may well assume, from the circumstance that, in the seventh dilution, it had very little or no effect; and that, even after the twenty-first day, when the Crotalus was omitted for too long an interval, the old symptoms of dry, parched tongue, the sopor, &c., would return with the same virulence; but, when the remedy was continued with perseverance, he again perspired in the night, and all the other symptoms improved.

On examining the symptoms of Crotalus, for the pur-

---

* The Crotalus, in order to produce its most powerful effect, must be taken from the snake in summer—if possible, immediately after catching it—and triturated with sugar of milk, and preserved in well-corked bottles. The preparation with alcohol, as is now well known, has very little or no effect.

pose of prescribing it in this disease, I found the similarity to the symptoms before me so great that a cer
tain involuntary conviction took possession of my mind
that this must be the remedy so long sought for. The
reason for its not acting promptly in the seventh dilution
was that, in such a severe disorder, larger doses ought
to be employed.* Moreover, if the virus of the Crotalus was not of some such high import, the use of this
class of animals could not very distinctly be seen. Besides it had already been extolled by several persons as
a superior remedy in this disease. In a letter from
New-Orleans, addressed to Dr. Bute, it was mentioned
as having cured two cases. A captain of a Brazilian
vessel always procured a stock of Crotalus before sail-
ing, alleging that it was the only reliable and sure
specific in yellow fever.

In 1857, Dr. José Luis Lorenzo Bablot Valdez, of
Cuba, furnished, in his inaugural dissertation, a very
minute comparison between the symptoms of yellow
fever and those obtained by the pathogenetic action of
Lachesis as well as Crotalus Horrid., and the similarity,
yes, absolute identity, is, indeed, very remarkable. Valdez instituted these comparisons in consequence of the experiments of a Dr. Humboldt, who, as we shall soon fully
detail below, inoculated, at Havana, the venom of some
serpent (supposed to be Crotalus) with a view of pre-

---

* That a dilution even one degree lower will often cure where
the one next to it has failed, has been corroborated to me lately in a
case of whooping cough, where the second dilution of Mephitis-putor
was only of slight benefit, but where the first dilution cured at once!

venting or modifying the yellow fever, in the same way as the vaccine virus is used for the prevention of small-pox.

What particularly struck me in this disease, and in which it differs from every other that ever fell under my observation, is its character of extreme obstinacy and treacherousness. Only malignant scarlatina is to be compared with it in this respect. There was no possible time to wait for the reaction of the medicine when the patient was better; but he required unremitting attention, and a continuance of the remedy every hour until the disease was totally subdued.

Every inch of ground had to be contested in this disease; for, when apparently entirely well, and the tongue had become moist, I omitted one night the continuance of the Crotalus; the next morning the tongue was dry and parched in the centre, and I was compelled to administer it every two hours, for several days, until he was cured.

Even after a decided improvement in his whole condition, and during the action of the Crotalus, which was continued all the time, he had, every other afternoon, a creeping sensation down the back and all over, followed by heat and perspiration.

During the first four days after his improvement commenced the patient was confined to oyster soup and different kinds of fruit, such as grapes, pears, &c., and these only in small quantities at a time, but often repeated. After the twenty-first day the appetite returned, and I had great difficulty in restraining it.

In every case the patients were ordered to have their

bed-linen changed every day, as well as their own clothing; and, as far as practicable, daily ablutions were per-
formed, and, I may say, not without very great and
visible advantage.

Several other cases, having all the unmistakable cha-
racteristics of the disease, were also chiefly or exclusively
cured by Crotalus, although they were of a milder nature.

2. Mrs. H.—*First day:* Felt an unpleasant chilly feeling.
Second day : Dragging pain in breast and lower part of
stomach (liver). The most characteristic symptom of
the disease was always this pain. *Third day :* Creepy
chills all day; nausea and vomiting of bile ; chilly feeling, alternating with heat, without the slightest perspiration; pain in the small of the back (region of kidneys) ; pain in the flesh all over. *Fourth day :* Drawing
pains in the knees, as if the joints were too short ; giddiness in the head; drowsiness, sleepiness, all the time ;
confusion of the head, saltish bitter taste in the mouth.
The second day the bowels were freely opened; since
then costive, no appetite. Since the first day no thirst;
water has not the right taste ; pulse 90. *Fourth day,*
P. M.: Sore pain beneath the left shoulder-blade to the
abdomen, where a swelling can be felt, and across the
region of the kidneys or loins. The region of the liver
is very sensitive to the touch; foul, fetid breath ; bitter
taste in the mouth.

Crotalus Horridus, 3, in water, repeated from one
to two hours, diminished the violence of the symptoms
from day to day, and entirely cured her in the space of
a week.

3. Mrs. R., in the same house as the above patient, was attacked on the twenty-first of October, at eleven o'clock, A. M., with the following symptoms: Darting, burning pains on the top and back of the head and over the eyes, shifting about; bewilderment of the brain; slight pain in the stomach and liver, and soreness in the right kidney; nausea and sickness of the stomach; constipation; fever, with the peculiar dry heat on the surface. Crotal. Horrid., 3, after aggravating all the above symptoms for a day, cured her on the third day. Afterwards she had severe shooting pains in the right hip, extending to the sacrum of the same side, with heat. These symptoms were evidently the result of the preceding fever, and were so obstinate and violent that a week elapsed before she was entirely cured of them.

4. D. P., aged fifteen.—The disease commenced on Friday afternoon with dull pain in the forehead, with weakness and pain all over. On Friday night the fever set in, for which his mother prescribed Bellad. On Saturday he was better all day; but in the night the fever returned, and he felt very nervous. On Sunday morning a swelling of the parotid glands ensued, and in the evening of the same day, at seven, P. M., bleeding from the right nostril, relieving the headache; after which dull pains over the right eye-brow set in; the nose and cheeks became red, face dark colored, hands almost black; constant inclination to pass water.

Fourth day: Continual drowsiness and sopor; sweetish taste in mouth; foul breath (the characteristic smell is more of a mouldy kind); great thirst; tongue dry in centre, point red and dry; attacks of light-headedness; sensation as if falling over a precipice; blisters on top of nose, with redness. This case was also cured by Crotalus, 2, in a few days.

5. Mrs. M.—The disease commenced, as usual, with a crawling sensation up and down the back, with chilliness all over in the afternoon, which lasted from five to six hours. Afterwards heat from head to foot; at the same time the head felt light and confused.

Severe tension and pressure on the top of the head, extending to the ears; soreness in the pit of the stomach to the left shoulder; pain in the bones.

Bowels at first relaxed, afterwards costive.

Yellow face, and tongue coated yellow; bitter taste in mouth; nausea; dull pain across the hips; aching pain in the centre of the chest to the back, shooting down to the arms and back of the head, and the whole spine; constant inclination to void urine, which is dark brown, almost black.

Crotalus Hor., 3, very quickly relieved all the above symptoms in a few days; but not a tickling dry cough in the centre of the chest, for which Stannum, 3, was prescribed with benefit.

Although the above, and several similar cases of the epidemic of 1853, attended by me, but not described here, had none of the severity which generally characterize the disease, they still showed some well-pronounced features common to them all; and, even in their apparent mildness, there was an obstinacy and inveteracy which are never met with in any other disease, and in which I could distinctly trace, even in this modified form, their relationship to the more malignant type of the disease, and to the same miasmatic cause. After the more violent symptoms of the disease had subsided there was a disposition to locate itself in some particular organ, as the right hypochondriac region or the liver, &c. I remarked that the right side was almost invariably this depository.

In 1858 there occurred not a few cases of genuine yellow fever in the city of Philadelphia, which, although they were of a milder and more modified type, could still be traced to this common source of infection.

I will here detail a few which may be comprised under this head, and which fell under my observation:

6. Mrs. B. came from Delaware with a disease which was supposed to be dumb ague, but which I would rather class among those anomalous cases of yellow fever, because some of the main symptoms were more similar to the yellow fever epidemic of 1853 than to the intermittent fevers of this neighborhood. The symptoms were: Chilliness, without thirst; pain all over the brain, as she expressed it, and not in any particular part; aching in region of liver and spleen, proceeding from right to left; diarrhœa, with much flatulency; much swelling across the stomach, with soreness to touch; headache during the chill and fever.

7. The above case, and that of her little son, H., similarly affected, were both cured by Crotalus Horridus, aided by Quinine, and, at a later period, Arsenicum. Both had the characteristic dirty yellow skin.

8. Pauline R., aged eight, had been sick for three days, with mouldy smell from mouth, tongue coated

white, very thirsty, pulse 100 ; sore, aching pain in region of liver; constipation of bowels; aching in forehead ; also, sore throat, yellowish, dirty complexion. This case was arrested in a few days by Crotalus Hor., second trituration, aided by Hippomanus-mancinella, exhibited alternately every hour.

9. The last case of the year 1858, and which proved fatal, was under allopathic treatment for three weeks without relief. The patient was not a regular drunkard, but a regular drinker; that is, he partook of six or seven glasses of brandy per day, which, as his friends truly averred, may be partly the cause of the fatal issue of the case. Bating his unfortunate drinking habits, he was a respectable man, much beloved by his friends and family. He contracted the disease on the wharf, where he had his place of business.

On my first visit I marked down the following symptoms : The disease commenced with aching in the back of the head and spasmodic pain in the stomach, for which large doses of Laudanum had been administered; after which he was attacked with severe pain in the back and violent headache.

Constant fever, with only slight or no perspiration, remitting somewhat in the morning, but returning with greater violence in the evening.

Wandering delirium.

Much thirst.

Constant drowsiness.

Mouth sore, as if he had been salivated.

The particular mouldy smell from the mouth.

No appetite. Tongue dry.

Four or five black, pappy evacuations a day before I was called in. The passages are now more natural.

The usual allopathic treatment was, Opium, Ipecac., Mercury, and then, again, Mercury and Opium.

After the exhibition of Crotalus, second trituration, in alternation with Arsenicum, all his symptoms improved: his tongue became moist, and, for some days, we thought he was well. On account of his typhoid symptoms, viz., perfect indifference—low delirium—I now interposed Rhus-tox., 2, in water; but all the symptoms were aggravated, and I again resorted to Crotalus and Arsenic, both of which seemed most analogous to his present state. He immediately improved; and the next day a warm perspiration broke out, the delirium ceased, and every one thought he would recover. But he now began to sink, and the tongue became dry again. Brandy and wine, in small quantities, with nourishment, barley-water, grapes, &c., did not prevent a fatal issue of the case. The reaction from the medicine and exhaustion from the disease were simultaneous. He could not rally. Death was the master, and closed the scene.

During the fatal epidemic at Norfolk, Virginia, I requested the late Dr. Campos, of that place, by letter, to employ the Crotalus Horridus, sending him a portion of it in triturations. He tried it in several instances, but without any beneficial results, as he avers.

A similar experience has been reported to me by Dr. Lingen, of Mobile, Alabama. He used different homœopathic remedies, according to the prominent indications, and with success. Of the Crotalus he saw no beneficial results. Other physicians in the South have been using the Crotalus with more or less success in this disease.

It is possible that the more severe cases can no more be benefitted by this remedy than by any other. Besides, if an improvement did not ensue very soon, in a dangerous and suddenly fatal disease like yellow fever, the physicians would feel themselves justified in changing the remedy at once for another. The forms of disease attended by me were all of a lighter kind, and, there-fore, more easily influenced by the remedy. I may re-mark, at the same time, that, in all cases, a decided benefit from the remedy was not perceptible until the second day. It had to be continued every hour for a day before reaction took place. The remedy ought to be exhibited on the first onset of the disease in order to be most useful and active. If the system is overpowered by the disorder no remedies will be able to rescue it.

CHAPTER VII.

COMPARISON OF THE SYMPTOMS OF YELLOW FEVER WITH THE PATHOGENETIC SYMPTOMS OF CROTALUS HORRIDUS.

WE will now compare the symptoms of the yellow fe-ver epidemic of 1853 with the *pathogenetic symptoms of Crotalus, contained in* "Jahr" (originally from C. Her-ing) and "Mure." Although some other descriptions of yellow fever symptoms might have been more complete, I have preferred to compare the Crotalus symptoms with Dr. Jewett's description of the symptoms of yellow fever, because it was during the *same* year I exhibited the Crotalus in ten slighter cases, several of which have been detailed above. Can there be a better fac-simile of yellow fever than the following *verbatim* extracts from the authentic pathogenesis of Crotalus?

GENERAL SYMPTOMS.

Languor and sudden decrease of vital force, with fever.—JAHR.

Yearly recurrence of blue-yellow spots, with swelling, pains, and fever.—JAHR.

Dr. Fellger, of Philadelphia, mentioned to me, as a well-authenticated fact, that Heinrich Witte, of Northampton County, Pennsylvania, fired a shot among hundreds of rattlesnakes copulating in the forest. After quitting the place without being bitten, from the mere deadly effluvium of so many snakes he had pains in the whole body, which became swollen, and also vertigo, lasting nearly nine months. Since then, *now ten years*, every year, about the same time, he has a return of the same symptoms. His skin *assumed a dirty-yellow* color, and has *remained so ever since.*

[The sister of O. P., the patient whose case we detailed before, was also attacked with the same disease, and similar symptoms to his own. She was cured in a short time by Crotalus and other remedies; but, a year afterwards, about the same time, she was again attacked by the very same disease, only with greater violence, and without the possibility of a fresh exposure. I am now convinced that it was the same disease slumbering in the system. Her parents thought so at the time. In her former attack she was chiefly treated and cured by Crotalus. In the returning disease the same remedy was again resorted to, and with benefit, but it soon lost its effect. Other remedies were exhibited without relief (Opium, &c.) Typhoid symptoms set in, and she died. She was always of a very weakly and delicate constitution.

One of the most remarkable instances occurring in my practice of the inveterate grasp with which the disease takes hold of individuals is the following: M. T. H. resided, four years ago, at Porto Rico, where he became attacked with yellow fever, treated allopathically, by bleeding, Quinine, &c. This was in the month of March. Now, every year, for four years, in the same month, whenever he smokes a segar in the evening, the same dry tongue, with the same headache as he experienced at Porto Rico, is excited and returns. Cold water and eating dissipate it.]

The symptoms return with greater violence after having remained quiet for two days. [This symptom is mentioned in "Jahr" as characteristic of Crotalus. In the last case of yellow fever which I attended there was nothing more characteristic than the suspension of the disease for a day or two, and its more violent return, without any particular cause than that of changing the medicine.]

Most of the symptoms appear on the right side.— JAHR. [*Highly characteristic of all the cases which came under my observation.*]

Trembling of the whole body.—JAHR.

MORAL AND MENTAL SPHERE.

Depression of spirits.—Mure. Delirium, with muttering.—Jahr.

HEAD.

Lancinations in the right temple; headache, as if the forehead would split, with weight above the eyes; pain under the right orbit and the right side of the forehead; sensitiveness of the hairy scalp on touching.—Mure.

EARS.

Deafness.—Mure.

EYES.

Redness of the eyes with lachrymation; yellow, faint, sunken eyes.—Jahr. Yellow rings around the eyes; dim, purulent look of the eye.

NOSE.

Discharge of bloody liquid from the nose.—Mure. Bleeding of the nose.—Mure.

FACE.

Flushes of heat in the face.—Mure. Yellow complexion.—Mure. Yellow face for a long while.—Jahr.

TONGUE.

Tongue of a scarlet red.—Mure. Brown, swollen tongue.—Jahr.

EPIGASTRIUM.

Pain in the stomach and pit of the stomach, with nausea and qualmishness; pressure in pit of stomach.—Jahr. Burning pinching at the pylorus.—Mure.

THIRST AND HUNGER.

Unquenchable, burning thirst.—JAHR. Thirst.—MURE. Fainting from hunger.—MURE.

TASTE, NAUSEA, AND VOMITING.

Sour taste. Rancid eructations. *Hiccough.*—JAHR. [This symptom, according to Dr. Holcombe, occurred in some bad cases.] *Nausea shortly after the bite.*—JAHR. Inclination to vomit, with cold skin. Vomiting; green, bilious, bitter, violent vomiting, every time he eats. Can only retain jelly, coffee, and a little brandy. [All these are from " Jahr."]

ABDOMEN.

Borborygmi.—MURE. The abdomen is sensitive.—MURE. Burning in the region of the liver.—JAHR. Constipation.—MURE. Yellowish diarrhœa.—MURE.

GENITO-URINARY ORGANS.

Emission of a deeply-colored urine.—MURE. Urine highly colored, red-yellow, as in jaundice.—JAHR. *Painful retention* of urine.—JAHR. Hæmorrhage from the urethra.—JAHR. Metrorrhagia (vermilion colored).—MURE. Lancinations in uterus.—MURE.

BACK.

Bruised pain in the back of the neck, from the larynx to the chin and lower teeth ; in sudden paroxysms.—JAHR. Drawing from the neck to the epigastrium.—MURE. Acute pain at the sacro-iliac articulation.—MURE. Painful heaviness in the loins.—MURE. Inter nal and contusive pain between the shoulders.—MURE.

EXTREMITIES.

Both in the symptoms of the lower as well as the upper extremities, produced by Crotalus, are to be found the crampy and other pains so characteristic of yellow fever; also cold feet.—MURE.

SLEEP.

Irresistible drowsiness, even at noon.—JAHR. Sopor. —JAHR. Somnolence the whole morning. Disposition to slumber.—MURE. Sleeplessness.—MURE. Dreams about dead persons and phantoms. Dreams about spiders attempting to crawl over her.—MURE.

FEVER AND PULSE.

Chilliness all over. Sense of chilliness.—MURE. Dry consumptive fever, with dry tongue and thirst. Constant fever, with thirst, bilious vomiting, palpitation of the heart, anguish, quick and feeble pulse, languor, and rapid sinking of the vital forces.—JAHR. Thirst during the fever. No sweat during the feverish warmth.—JAHR. Pulse from 100 to 130.—JAHR. Pulse feeble and quick, with fever and languor. Pulse first hard, then quick, then feeble and slow. Tremulous imperceptible pulse, with loss of motion and speech.—JAHR. Pulse 98 to 104.—MURE.

SKIN.

Red pimples all over. Pimples resembling flea-bites, afterwards becoming raised and exfoliating, leaving a black point in the centre.—MURE. Blisters and livid spots on the body, with frequent fainting fits and imperceptible pulse.—JAHR.

Bright yellow spots on upper part of right hand.—
MURE.

Black spots over the whole body.—JAHR.   Yellow
spots over the whole body.—JAHR.

The whole body and urine look yellow, as in jaundice.
—JAHR. The skin is covered with little blotches.—JAHR.

CASES OF BILIOUS REMITTENT FEVER.

Besides the slighter cases of yellow fever, severe cases
of *bilious remittent fever*, prevailing in Philadelphia
and its vicinity during the same years, were either
cured by Crotalus Horridus alone, or, at least, very much
aided by it, as the following cases will testify:

1. Mrs. R. walked out, late in October, in a district where
fevers from the Schuykill River often prevail, and contracted the disease. She was a robust lady, of florid complexion, and hardly ever sick. She had the peculiarity
of not perspiring, even in the hottest weather.

When called to see her, on the twenty-first of October,
the following symptoms presented themselves: On
taking a long breath, cough and pain on the right
side of the chest, with tickling and expectoration of
tough white mucus. We mention these symptoms first
because they were the most troublesome, and she complained of them more than any others; but the main
disease was the bilious remittent fever, with the following symptoms: Pulse from 130 to 140, the fever remitting towards evening and midnight, but never entirely abating; delirious; circumscribed redness on both

4

cheeks; constant thirst; chilliness on drinking; fœtid breath; peculiar mouldy smell from the mouth, which characteristic symptom we have observed in the re-mittent fevers of this climate; fœtid diarrhœa and in-voluntary evacuations; great apathy. The above com-prised the chief symptoms.

The cough was relieved by Laurocerasus and Lactuca-virosa, after first prescribing Phosphor. and Sulph. with-out success.

The remittent fever was not at all affected by them. Chamomilla, subsequently prescribed, merely caused a mitigation of the symptoms. It was only after the use of the *Crotalus Horrid.*, 2, that the fever abated. The action was so prompt and energetic that it made a strong impression at the time upon my mind.

The tincture of *Leontodon-taraxacum* is the only re-medy which I saw act equally prompt in other cases of bilious fever. The cases in which Taraxacum was pre-ferred were characterized by the following symptoms: Tongue peeling off in patches, leaving a dark red spot underneath; tongue was never dry; bitter taste in the mouth, with nausea, and often bilious vomiting; always great fullness and heaviness in the forehead; oppression of the chest, with affection of the kidneys. There were of course, other symptoms, according to the peculiarity of the constitution, but the above were common to them all.

2. During a temporary sojourn in the country Mr. H. was attacked by a malignant intermittent fever, gradu-ally verging into the remittent type. The attending homœopathic physician prescribed, from August 17th to

August 28th, 1857, the following remedies, with only partial success: 1. Bryonia, 6, Arsenic, 6; 2. Phosph., 1, Acon., 3; 3. China; 4. Cocculus, 6, Merc.-sol., 3; 5. Ipecac., 6, Bellad., 6; 6. Nux-v., 6; 7. Bellad., 6; 8. Bellad., 30; 9. Taraxacum, 2; 10. Nux-v., 6, Acon., 3; 11. Stram., 9, Ars., 3; 12. Hyoscyam., 6; 13. Bellad., 6, Arsenic, 3; 14. Quinine-sulph., $\frac{1}{10}$; 15. Bellad., 6, Ipec., Tart.-em.; 16. Ipecac., Nux-v.; 17. Taraxacum, Arsen., $1\frac{1}{2}$, Tart.-em., $\frac{1}{10}$; 18. Tinct. Taraxacum.

After my return, on examining the patient, I noted down the following symptoms: The fever set in at first with a violent chill, followed by severe fever and perspiration all night; mouldy foul smell from the mouth; centre of tongue dry, sides moist and whitish. Accompanying the fever there was vomiting of the food, without taste; urine thick yellowish-brown. After the first chill there was only fever at four, P. M., followed by perspiration at night, and the other symptoms as mentioned; also rigidity of the left side of the neck.

This severe remittent fever was rapidly cured by Crotalus Horridus, 1 and 2, taken for several days. The Crotalus removed all the above symptoms: a few doses of Quinine finished the cure.

3. Another cure by Crotalus, 3, is the following: Miss —— had fever every afternoon, followed by coldness and shivering in the back, without subsequent perspiration, except in the hands. She also had nausea, violent headache, and pain in the back, and thirst during the fever; restless morning sleep, with eyes half open, also mouth open; pain in the bowels. In this

case Eupatorium-perf. had been exhibited, at first with partial success.

The following additional cases, resembling yellow fever, or the more malignant bilious typhoid type, may also be mentioned here :

4. This case was more important, on account of the peculiar character of the symptoms, and their great severity, than any striking action of remedies. It was evidently a case of malignant bilious fever ; and, after the patient's death, the whole body, and particularly the face, assumed a complete yellow color.

When I was called in to attend the case, with two other homœopathic physicians, the predominating symptoms were the loquacious delirium, with a desire to escape out of bed. The tongue was yellowish brown, and dry in the centre ; the lips sore and cracked ; and there were sordes on the teeth. Stramonium, whose pathogenesis seemed similar to the above symptoms, was exhibited with the greatest benefit. The delirium and wildness were all gone the next day, but the symptoms returned with renewed violence. New specifics, selected according to their affinities, seemed at first to exert a very beneficial effect, but afterwards failed. Crotalus was one of these remedies, but gave only slight relief. As the disease advanced, the pulse sank. As usual, stimulants, like wine, were resorted to ; but what could they avail ? They could only rouse the flickering life for a moment.

A grand and strong nature had prematurely exhausted itself, owing to its ignorance of physiological laws. Excesses in *Bacho* and *Venere*, and in the most extreme style, had done the deed. The system was, as it were, prepared for years to absorb such a disease, under which it had to succumb, as of a necessity, because there were no stamina left.

5. Miss ——, fourteen years of age, had even a more severe attack of the same disease than the foregoing; but, her constitution being still sound, a cure was not impossible. It was attained with great difficulty.

A year before Miss ——'s brother had the yellow fever, at least his disease resembled very much the epidemic which then prevailed under the name of yellow fever. A year later, just before her own attack, Mary, her sister, was affected by a very similar disease. The question may fairly be asked, Can the yellow fever contagion remain, in a dormant or inactive state, a whole year in a house, and then, when favored by the state of the atmosphere, be resuscitated, and infect susceptible constitutions exposed to it? This question deserves our most serious consideration. I do not say that both these cases, recurring a year after the first one, were positively yellow fever, but they certainly resembled the disease very much.

The first symptoms marked down on the appearance of the disease were as follows:

1. For several days continual fever; tongue streaked yellowish brown in the centre, dry and rough.

2. Pain over the eyes.

3. Constant bilious discharges.

4. Appetite voracious.

5. Perspiration, without abating the fever.

6. Occasionally chills.

7. Throat swelling internally.

8. Skin yellow.

After Crotalus Horridus, 3, all the symptoms improved, except No. 1. At the same time the skin became dry, and remained so until the termination of the disease.

September 27th, 1855, five days later, the case presented the following symptoms: Tongue dry, brown, and cracked in the centre, swollen, moist, and white on the margin; deep red across the point, and dry; dryness of the throat; no desire for water, although the mouth was dry and she had to moisten it; nose bleeds a little all the time; tenderness in the left hypochondrium (after Phosph.-ac. the pain went to the right hypochondrium); after eating oranges the fœtid smell disappeared and gave place to an acid one; yellowish, watery, bilious passages four to six times a day; no appetite whatever; suppression of urine, passed only the slightest quantity, of the color of brandy; morning aggravation gradually changing into an evening exacerbation; dizziness on raising herself up; continual drowsiness; mind dull and wandering during sleep; pulse 136.

The following remedies relieved, but did not cure the symptoms appended to them:

Opium: Tongue dry, cracked in the centre; constant drowsiness; tenderness in the left hypochondrium; want of thirst. Opium also reduced the pulse to 100.

Belladonna, 3 (aided by Chamomilla): Swollen tongue; drowsiness; suppression of urine. Produced, also, slight perspiration.

Crotalus: Suppression of urine; constant drowsiness.

Stramonium: Swollen, dry, cracked tongue; no desire for water, although her mouth is dry and she has to moisten it; suppression of urine; lying on the right side; pain when she lies on the left. (After Stramonium she could lie on either side.)

Muriatic-acid, 3 : Disposition to slip down in bed; soreness of the right hypochondrium on contact; swelling of the tongue.

The last and final portrait of the disease was taken October 12th, 1855, and is as follows: Pain and heat behind both ears and back part of the head; (it was very difficult to discover the nature of the pain and its locality, as the patient was speechless, very deaf, and almost blind) ; deafness, difficulty of speaking; every evening cold hands and feet; pulse 120; circumscribed redness on left cheek (the family, on both sides, are consumptive;) great thirst for cold water, formerly aversion to it; tongue rough and dry; picking of the nose; great apathy and restlessness ; delirium, wildness, and disposition to get out of bed; gritting of teeth when half asleep, not when fully awake. (The gritting of the teeth consisted in a spasmodic contraction and drawing backwards of the lower jaw. The mother discovered the true nature of this symptom by putting her finger in the mouth of the patient, when she began to bite by elevating the lower jaw. She has naturally a protruding upper lip and teeth.) Perverseness, will not take food.

The action of the different remedies during the above state may be summed up thus:

Hyoscyamus had the happiest effect on the gritting

of the teeth, it also improved the tongue and voice (which was very high pitched and shrill, with much incoherent talk); apathy; pulse went down to 108.

Crotalus and *Hyoscyamus :* Both were instrumental in curing the pain in the back of the head. They relieved the difficulty in speaking, picking of nose; *particularly*, also, the restlessness, wildness, delirium, and disposition to escape, as well as the gritting of the teeth, and spasmodic contraction of the lower jaw.

Crotalus alone : The dryness, roughness, and swelling of the tongue.

Nux-vomica and *Arsenic*, next to Stramonium and Hyoscyam. had the best effect in bringing back the voice.

Arsenicum caused the appetite to return, and produced sleep at night. After its exhibition the evening fever receded to one, P. M.

Rhus-toxicodendron finally subdued the fever entirely, and removed the redness and dryness of the tongue. When, after some time, the redness returned, *Oleum Jecinoris-aselli* had the most permanent effect. All these remedies were exhibited in the lower dilutions.

6. Late in September I was called, in consultation, to see a case of typhoid remittent fever at Frankford, six miles from Philadelphia. The patient had been treated, with varying success, by the attending physician, for two months, the disease returning several times after weekly intermissions. It had commenced with chills, a characteristic sore pain from pit of stomach to region of liver, with qualmishness and nausea, slight delirium,

most violent pain in the back of the neck and back on the least motion. On the first attack the pain was more in the back of the neck and back, but the second time it affected more the front and side region of the liver. Complete sleeplessness.

Crotalus Horrid., 2, had also, in this case, a decidedly and immediately beneficial effect: the patient expressing his feelings about the beneficial action of the remedy. Subsequently an abscess of the liver formed, which was successfully treated by Hepar-sulph., 2. The patient entirely recovered.

7. A remittent fever—in the case of the mayor of a neighboring town—very similar in its symptoms to the above, in consultation with another homœopathic physician, was immediately relieved, and finally entirely cured by means of Crotalus Horridus, 2, in alternation with Arsenicum. These two remedies very often alternated beneficially in similar cases.

8. In the beginning of this summer (1860) I was called to see Miss T. E., who had already suffered for some time with a violent headache and fever, for which a Belladonna plaster had been prescribed.

This plaster violently aggravated the symptoms, and she had to remove it. When I subsequently saw her the following symptoms were noted down: There were two distinct paroxysms of fever daily, one early in the morning and the other at seven, P. M. At first these paroxysms were preceded by slight chilliness, but not afterwards. The most prominent symptoms accompanying these fevers were violent pain and heaviness in the bones of the forehead and back of the head; also throbbing in the vertex, with pain in the back and region of the liver, followed by a continual yellowish-brown watery diarrhœa. There was also a sensation of excoriation in the centre of the chest, with coughing and white expectoration. Complete sleeplessness and flightiness every night. During the fever the skin was always dry, with redness of the right cheek, and not followed by perspiration; the tongue was whitish; complete loss of appetite.

As the patient particularly complained about the headache, and the ordinary remedies, as Belladonna, Aconite, &c., remained without effect, I gave her the Veratrum-viride, which relieved the head and somewhat abated the fever, but only for a short time.

After Crotalus Horrid., 2, in water, the fever, for the first time, did not return in the morning; the pulse, which always had been over 130, lowered to 80; perspiration also commenced. She had the first good night's rest for weeks, and in less than a week entirely recovered without any other remedy.

9. The power of Crotalus has been exemplified to me quite recently in a severe case of bilious remittent fever. V. A., aged ten, returned from the country on the twenty-first of July, with a fever, for which Aconite was prescribed by the mother. As this fever did not yield to her domestic efforts, I was sent for on the twenty-fifth of July, when the following portrait of disease presented itself: During the first few days the fever was preceded by some chills, but not followed by perspiration; afterwards there was only fever, with hot skin, without the slightest perspiration. There were two de-

cided paroxysms of fever, one in the morning, about eight o'clock, and the other from five to seven, P. M., which last continued for some time after the morning fever had entirely ceased. There was also this characteristic symptom, that the patient complained of being chilly during the fever.

The other symptoms were: Great heat and aching in the forehead, also pain on the top and back of the head; the right side of the back of the neck was painful for a whole week; foul breath; tongue coated yellow, with enlargement of the papillæ; constant thirst for cold water, with nausea and sick stomach; aching pain in the region of the liver and stomach; total want of appetite, even aversion to food; pain in the bones of both legs, particularly at night; great restlessness and fretfulness. Aconite, Eupator.-perf., Veratr.-viride, and Gelseminum semper. had but a slight effect in arresting the progress of the disease. Rhus-radicans, which was selected after a careful study of the symptoms, seemed to mitigate them all; but it did not prevent the tongue from becoming brown, and afterwards quite black. There was also sopor, with increase of heat in the forehead.

All these symptoms clearly pointed to Crotalus Hor., which was prescribed in the second trituration, and with its usual happy effect. The sides of the tongue became moist, the violence of the fever and the thirst diminished, the sopor also disappeared, and the little patient asked, for the first time, for some food, which consisted of grapes and peaches. It should be remarked here that, from the first exhibition of the Crotalus, five or six bilious passages became the order of the day for a week, after which they subsided. The black coating on the tongue only very gradually improved. The last patch was removed by the busy fingers of the little patient herself.—Here was a violent fever, which often lasts from four to six weeks, entirely cured in fourteen days!

10. M. H. was lately sent by his father, residing in Memphis, Tennessee, to this city, in order to be cured of a very obstinate bilious remittent fever, which the largest doses of Quinine were only partially able to subdue.

In the beginning of his sickness there was some chilliness, but afterwards there was only heat every night, with violent aching pain and burning heat in the forehead, accompanied by nausea. The tongue was coated yellowish white and was sometimes dry; there was also considerable pain in the bowels. He had the peculiar dirty-yellow complexion, and was very much emaciated; skin dry.

My first prescription was Nux-vomica and Eupatorium-perf., both in the second trituration. His general health became better, but these remedies were not able to arrest the evening fever. Crotalus Horridus, second trituration, three times a day, removed the fever the second day. His complexion became totally changed, and he almost looked like a new being. Another package of Crotalus Horridus, 2, three times a day, completed the cure, and he returned to Memphis entirely well.

A P P E N D I X.

——

CHAPTER VIII.

NICOLAS MANZINI'S HISTORY OF THE PROPHYLACTIC EF-
FECTS OF INOCULATION AGAINST THE YELLOW FEVER,
AS PRACTICED BY ORDER OF THE SPANISH GOVERN-
MENT AT THE MILITARY HOSPITAL, HAVANA.

THE positive value of Crotalus is further corroborated
by Manzini's history of the inoculation of the venom
of some serpent,* for the prevention of yellow fever, at
Havana, in the year 1854, by a Dr. Humboldt.

In the month of October, 1854, Dr. William Lam-
bert de Humboldt, residing in New-Orleans, wrote to
General Don José de la Concha, Governor of the island
of Cuba, that he had discovered a substance which
would serve as a preventative of yellow fever. This
substance, whose principle consisted of the venom of a
serpent, would afford protection against this formidable
disease by inoculation, in the case of strangers visiting
the locality where yellow fever prevailed epidemically.

He had already practiced, in New-Orleans, his inoculation with success, having, during a period of

---

* There is now little doubt but that this was the Crotalus Horridus.

nine years, inoculated 1438 individuals, of which number only seven were attacked by yellow fever, and two died.

After a consultation with the medical faculty the Governor invited Humboldt to Havana, placing a ward of the Military Hospital under his absolute control.

Mr. Humboldt had hardly arrived in Havana when Dr. Manzini sought his acquaintance, feeling interested in a man who, like himself, had made tropical fevers the subject of his studies. He found Humboldt a man of about thirty-six years of age, of tuberculous feeble constitution, but full of fire and enthusiasm for his new enterprise. Humboldt spoke four languages, but his medical education, with the exception of his knowledge of fevers, seems to have been imperfect. He, like Manzini, believed that the epidemic remittent fevers of tropical countries and yellow fever were identical; they only differed in degree.* Humboldt subsequently died at Vera Cruz.

Although this discovery is derived from a person whose identity, according to Manzini, is somewhat doubtful, and whose character is not free from objection, it may still be, as some other discoveries of doubtful origin, of the highest importance to humanity, deserving our most serious consideration; the more so if, as Manzini maintains, the inoculation was, on the whole, successful.

Humboldt was led to his discovery by observing that galley-slaves, brought from Mexico to Vera Cruz, who had been bitten by some viper on the way, always had decided symptoms of yellow fever.

---

* This is also my opinion.—C. N.

To all the inoculated Humboldt administered, at the same time, a syrup of Mikamia-guaco, the well-known antidote to all snake poisons. The Spanish Committee of the University, consisting of Drs. Cowley, Castroverde, and Benjumeda, under the supposition that the symptoms of the inoculation might be owing to the syrup of Mikamia-guaco, demanded of him to exhibit the Guaco separately, and to inoculate, as a counter-proof, some animals to whom the Mikamia was not administered. This proposition was rejected, on the ground that the gentlemen of the Committee had no knowledge of the researches of the two Vargas, Abreu de Lima, Mutis, Bertero, Humboldt and Bonpland, Sigaud and Rusz, with regard to the pathogenetic and therapeutic properties of Guaco; that they ignored what was said of the venom of serpents from Lucian to our times; and, finally, forget the results obtained by Fontana, Russell, Blot, Fanau de la Cour, Guyon, and Rusz, from the inoculation of these poisons into the cellular tissue. Humboldt likewise declined the proposition of Dr. Castroverde, to have a certain quantity of the virus diluted, in order to experiment with it according to the rules of homœopathy.

The news of this inoculation produced a great sensation among the people; they considered it analogous to vaccination—to the discovery of Jenner—and every one persuaded himself that some means was now found to stem the current of this pestilence, and to make these regions inhabitable for the new emigrant.

Intrinsically considered, the inoculation fulfilled its promises, and produced phenomena analogous to yellow fever, just as vaccination produces symptoms similar to small-pox. Dr. Manzini relinquished his practice, in order to devote himself entirely to this "immense scientific question." He himself inoculated some two thousand, and his faith increased every day.

Notwithstanding the inoculation a great number of the inoculated were attacked by the fever, which was treated with success, by himself and Humboldt, by his new (?) method, which consisted : 1. In bleedings from the feet, to the relaxation of the sphincter-ani muscle; 2. Large doses of Quinine and Calomel. In the majority of cases the disease was cured in from twelve to forty-eight hours. Out of three hundred and thirty-three cases of these fevers only one death occurred.

[Might not all these fevers, in a great measure, have been avoided by a more diluted inoculation, or by administering the inoculating matter internally, in small doses ?—C. N.]

The Asiatic cholera made its appearance in July, when there were 134 cases ; during August there were 252. Dr. Manzini alludes to the intimate connection of yellow fever and cholera, the second stage of the former of which often degenerated into the latter. *Among the inoculated the cholera was very rare*, the inoculation acting indirectly as a preservative.

After the cessation of the cholera, in September, yellow fever again made its appearance, but more frequently and with greater severity among the uninoculated than among the inoculated. One cause of the success of the inoculation not having been so striking he ascribes to the unhealthy position of the Military Hospital.

Mr. Bastareche, the chief military Health Officer for the island of Cuba, made a report on the inoculation. According to Manzini, he ought to have been more minute. If his aim was to come to a definite conclusion he ought to have stated how many soldiers were attacked according to the different periods of their residence at Havana, the influence of a first attack on the subsequent ones, the extreme limit of the febrile acclimation, the proportion of mortality among those who had been attacked, the influence of the locality, &c. For the purpose of arriving at a safe conclusion all these points ought to have been regarded by Mr. Bastareche. He did not do so, and contradicted himself in his report.

A month after these experiments had been conducted, when Dr. Manzini had ceased to be connected with the Hospital, it was reported to him that there were great losses among the inoculated, and, at the end of the year 1855, the inoculation was pronounced a total failure.

With regard to the *inoculation itself*, Mr. Humboldt gives the following data:

The inoculation has no effect upon individuals who are acclimated in the places where the yellow fever prevails. It exerts the greatest power on strangers recently arrived, and according to the susceptibility of their constitutions to the inroads of yellow fever. In order to exercise its preservative virtue it is not necessary to produce violent symptoms. With those not affected by the first inoculation it may be repeated.

5

There were two phenomena to which Manzini paid particular attention : the decrease of the pulse and the hæmorrhagic tendency of the gums. He looked upon this decrease of the pulse as a lowering of the vitality of the foreigner, placing his temperament in harmony with the influences of the new climate; in the hæmorrhagic tendency of the gums he saw the pathognomonic sign of yellow fever. The hæmorrhage from the gums is only the first symptom of the black vomit. On this account the disease has been compared with the scurvy by Pouppé-Desportes, Campet, Términ, Dalmas, Valentin, Tood, Chabert, Pugnet, Robert, Kéraudren, and Demadrid.

The first physician who observed this phenomenon of the gums, and who established it in a memoir on the subject, was Dr. Francois Xavier Loro, of Cadiz.

It has been supposed that the hæmorrhage, swelling, and inflammation were owing to the almost general use of Calomel; but it has been observed in many cases where Calomel was never used, and also long before the Calomel practice came into vogue. Many other writers have considered it as a characteristic symptom of yellow fever, such as Gérardin and Gros, Dariste, Ardévol, Catel, and Rusz, also Saravesi and Saint Esprit. The latter mentions twenty-two cases, in the same year (1856), with the hæmorrhage of the gums, none of which proved fatal.

These symptoms of the gums may therefore be considered as the pathognomonic phenomena of the initiatory period of the yellow fever, and, according to Manzini, the most certain of all, for the black vomit does not exist in the majority of cases.

In reviewing the whole question, he cites about as many medical men who do *not* consider the hæmorrhage of the gums as characteristic of yellow fever as those who are of that opinion. He himself comes finally to the conclusion that the inflammation or hæmorrhage from the gums is not a certain diagnostic symptom of yellow fever, as it is also observed at the commencement of other diseases, *e. g.*, small-pox, measles, &c.

The fact is, it seems to me, that a single symptom cannot furnish a sure diagnosis of any disease. We must take cognizance of all phenomena in order to form a correct conclusion.

The symptoms of the inoculation appeared in the following order:

At the moment of the inoculation there was vertigo, which soon passed away. There was also a nervous trembling, which is rarer, but which lasts a longer time.

After seven hours the pulse is permanently modified: it is either too frequent or too slow, stronger or weaker.

In eleven hours there is febrile heat.

At the end of fourteen hours, headache, want of appetite, thirst. At the end of sixteen hours, red countenance, injection of the conjunctiva, epiphora.

The swelling of the gums is observed from the commencement, to which are added slight colic-pains produced by the remedy (*Guaco*), which the patient has taken immediately after the inoculation.

1. At the expiration of 18 hours, pain in the gums,

the margins of which redden around the teeth; pain of the salivary glands and in the direction of the different nervous branches of the face and teeth.

2. In 19 hours, pains in the lower jaw and in the direction of the submaxillary nerve, lassitude.

3. In 20 hours, bitter taste, drowsiness, coryza, and œdema of the face.

4. In 22 hours, constrictive sensation of the throat, without a visible alteration of the mucous membrane.

5. In 23 hours, yellow jaundice.

6. In 24 hours, hæmorrhage of the gums.

7. In 28 hours, yellowness of the sclerotic coat of the eyes, shivering.

8. In 29 hours, angina-tonsillaris.

9. In 30 hours, pain in the kidneys.

10. In 36 hours, swelling of the eye-lids.

11. In 38 hours, pain of the muscles and joints.

12. In 40 hours, toothache.

13. In 72 hours, swelling of the lower lip.

At different hours, sensual excitements.

During convalescence, itching of the cuticle, cutaneous eruptions of various kinds.

SPECIAL OBSERVATIONS OF MANZINI ON THE SYMPTOMS OF THE INOCULATED.

As a kind of antidote to the often too great violence of the symptoms Humboldt administered to his patients, *immediately after the inoculation*, a syrup, composed principally of the Mikamia-guaco and Rhubarb, with some Iodide of Potash and Gamboge.*

---

* The exhibition of such a mixture, as it would materially modify

In one case bleeding had to be resorted to.

The inoculated, having a yellow tongue on the fifth day, had to take Citrate of Magnesia.

The surest antidote to the symptoms of the inoculated was the administration of the Sulphate of Quinine.

PULSE.—In the majority of cases the inoculation produced a diminution in the frequency of the pulse, and, what was most remarkable, the sixty-eight who showed this diminution were precisely those who had the most frequent pulse before being inoculated, and those who showed an acceleration had formerly only 69 pulsations in a minute. All this can, of course, be explained on the principle of reaction. According to Manzini, on giving due weight to both series of phenomena, they would, on an average, amount to 27 pulsations in a minute.

This diminution of the frequency of the pulse is the most common phenomenon of the inoculation, and exists in proportion to its acceleration as sixty-two to twelve.

The decrease in the force of the pulse is also very marked. Nearly all cases show at one time a very noticeable feebleness and sinking alternating with its acceleration, each lasting six hours on an average.

HEADACHE.—The headache is one of the most common symptoms of the inoculation.

It lasts, on an average, twenty-one hours.

It can exist without any alteration of the pulse.

---

the symptoms of the inoculation, was, to say the least of it, perfectly absurd. If the inoculation acted too powerfully, why was not a dilution of the matter made with milk, or some other innocuous substance ?—C. N.

It generally occupies the frontal and orbital region of the head.

HEAT.—The heat does not seem to be owing to the increase of the pulse. It was even perceived in those cases where the pulse sank.

THROAT.—The deglutition was difficult in all cases, and the tongue was more or less coated.

CUTICLE.—After the cessation of the more acute symptoms it was very common to witness an itching of the skin, of which the inoculated complained very much.

Another group of phenomena constituted the neuralgic pains in the head and neck.

In many cases there were observed erections at night.

NUMERICAL RECAPITULATION.

The circulation was modified in 183 out of 187
Headache had existed in . . . 160   "   187
The face was changed in . . . 54   "   74
The gums were affected in . . 74   "   74
Colics existed in 52   "   74
Swellings of salivary glands in 5   "   74
Pain in the lower jaw present in 10   "   74
Lassitude in 59   "   74
Drowsiness in 10   "   74
Coryza in 16   "   74
Bitter taste in 54   "   74
Spasm of the throat in . . . 14   "   74
Jaundice in 16   "   74
Frost in 13   "   74
Heat in 46   "   74
Perspiration in 17   "   74
Angina-tonsillaris in 17   "   74
Pains in muscles and joints in 7   "   74

The intermittent character of several of the symptoms produced by the inoculation is one of the most interesting and important points. It is now clearly established, in the excellent work of the illustrious Chervin, that the nature of all fevers arising from marsh miasma is very similar, if not the same.*

NATURE OF THE INOCULATION.

After comparing the analogous effects of the venom of serpents, as published by various authors, with those of the inoculated, Manzini finds them very similar. He does not pretend to say which snake poison Dr. Humboldt used for his inoculation. It is also strange, although no follower of Hahnemann, that he does not consider the similarity of action of the poison and the yellow fever as an objection to its use.

Among the remarkable phenomena cited are several proclaiming the long continuance of the effects from the bite. The naturalist Lesueur felt his sufferings for ten years after having been bitten by a Crotalus Horridus, and H. Cloquet says that men who have been bitten by a venomous serpent suffer all their lives. Koster reports the case of a Negro who was bitten by a rattlesnake, and experienced all his life pains in the limbs, which always returned at the period of the full moon.†

---

* This may, perhaps, explain why I have found Crotalus so useful in certain bilious and remittent fevers.—C. N.

† It will be seen that the above facts correspond with my own experience, as expressed in a previous chapter, that yellow fever, ike the effects of Crotalus, may return in the same person a whole

The symptoms produced by these poisons would have been found still more analogous if their effects had been observed with more care and accuracy. Manzini quotes from Dr. Mure's work the pathogenetic symptoms of the Crotalus-cascavella and Elaps-corallinus, which show great similarity to Humboldt's inoculation.

I.—*Results of the Inoculation.*

From the foregoing facts the author arrives at the conclusion that the inoculations produce a portrait of the principal and most important phenomena of the yellow fever. These consist of an expression of countenance of a peculiar kind, similar to that of the eruptive fevers, to which is joined an appearance of drunkenness, particularly shown in the eyes, which are injected; after which comes the headache and pain in the loins, the changes in the gums, and, later, the jaundice, the hæmorrhages, and suppression of urine. These are among the most constant of the innumerable phenomena of this terrible disease.

To the above we must briefly add the announcement of Humboldt, that the effects of the inoculation were more severe in proportion to the elevation of the temperature, and that they were manifested most distinctly with new-comers. On the other hand, there were some who felt no effects whatever from the inoculation. These consisted of persons who had resided a long time

---

year after having been subject to the disease, and without being exposed to a fresh infection.—C. N.

in the country, as well as such as had only recently arrived. They only had a little headache on the third day, or a slight pain in the loins.

Out of twenty inoculated individuals, who had already been subject to yellow fever, thirteen were attacked by the principal symptoms of the inoculation.

A microscopic examination of the blood taken from the gums of an inoculated person showed elliptic globules; they were not rounded off, and preserved their color. Another time, in the urine of another person, he found them deformed and rounded. It may be observed, however, that this same deformity has been noticed in diseases of an entirely different nature, particularly in Bright's disease.

II.—*Number of Inoculated Individuals at the Military Hospital, and the conditions of their acclimation in relation to the time of residence and the diseases they had undergone.*

From the eighteenth of December, 1854, to the twenty-eighth of June 1855, 2,477 individuals had been inoculated: 1214 belonging to the army, and 1263 to the royal navy.

The conditions of their acclimation, in relation to the time of their residence in America, were the following:

TABLE No. I.—LENGTH OF TIME THE INOCULATED HAD
RESIDED IN THE ISLAND OF CUBA.

For 13 years 1
" 11 "   2
" 10 "   1
"   9 "   2
"   8 "   9
"   7 "   5
"   6 "   6
"   5 "   13
"   4 "   15
"   3 "   41
"   2 "   168
    1 year 249
" six months 587
" several days 1378
                                ——
    Total 2,477

In reference to the febrile diseases with which they
had been attacked before the inoculation, during their
residence in America, the 2,477 inoculated may be
classed as follows :

TABLE No. II.—NUMBER OF INDIVIDUALS.

Ephemeral fevers 73
Intermittent "   73
Remittent   "   33
Cholera-morbus 5
Small-pox 3
Acute inflammation with the fever . . . 25
                                    ——
    Total 212

These 212 diseases have been distributed as follows :

TABLE No. 3.

Series of	13	years	—no disease.				
"	11	"	1 intermittent fever.				
"	9	"	1 ephemeral	"			
"	8	"	1 ephemeral and 1 intermittent fever.				
"	7	"	1	"	2	"	fevers.
"	5	"	1	"	2	"	"
"	4	"	3	"	3	"	"
"	3	"	10	"	4	"	"
"	2	"	8	"	5	"	"

All the other cases of fever took place during the first eighteen months of the residence of the individuals in the island of Cuba or in its sea-ports. The 1378 (as mentioned before) only had not been affected with any disease for several days.

III.—Every one was inoculated, except where the prodromi of a fever were already present, which falsely might be ascribed to the inoculation.

A lady with a very painful neuralgia, the remains of a very pernicious Chagres fever, found herself cured after the inoculation.

The inoculation exerts an injurious influence upon the tuberculous. It seems to promote the softening of the tubercles. In speaking of the nature of the inoculation, hæmorrhage was mentioned as one of the symptoms produced by the bite of venomous serpents.

Dr. Manzini also remembers the case of a mariner, who, immediately after the inoculation, was attacked by pneumonia, with an expectoration like dried prunes, as is the case during mortification of the lungs. He was sick for a long time, but was finally cured.

In the case of a Sister of Charity, inoculated, there

was a complete pleurisy, with a fever of a remittent type.

Nothing, however, was of higher interest than the fevers from which the inoculated suffered. They resembled yellow fever in its initiatory stage. Nothing was wanting—expression of countenance, pain in the loins, headache, the symptoms of the gums; and those fevers which made their appearance in such an alarming manner did not last longer, in five out of seven cases, than from twelve to forty-eight hours. They were all treated by Manzini, by what he calls his method, which was as follows: Venesection by the foot until relaxation of the sphincter-ani. Half an hour afterwards sixty grains of Sulphate of Quinine and sixty grains of Calomel, in three packages, one every hour in black coffee. The Sulphate of Quinine to be continued in the same dose every two hours during the intensity of the fever; an emollient enema, every six hours, of knot-grass water (polygonum aricularo); finally, the headache and pain in the loins was combatted by scarifying cuppings, and the Calomel repeated. The repetition of the general bleeding is to be avoided when it continues to rain much.

Notwithstanding this absurd treatment, the success of the inoculation, if we may believe Manzini, was quite favorable. But I must again aver my opinion that, if the inoculating virus had been exhibited internally in a small dose to the unacclimated, as a preventative, the symptoms of yellow fever would have been much milder, and not have required the violent and active medical treatment described above.

Be that as it may, out of the 701 inoculated at the

Military Hospital, 121 were pronounced as having been attacked by yellow fever, of which 47 died. This is the report of the committee appointed by Mr. Baste-reche in behalf of the Government. The chairman of this committee was Mr. Gutierrez, sometimes Mr. Benjumeda. According to Manzini, the remaining 580 cases had also symptoms of the fever, which fully entitle them to be ranked among the yellow fever cases. They were placed under the influence of Quinine, and rarely lasted more than forty-eight hours. They very much resembled in their character the remittent fevers to which the Creoles or old colonists are subject who remain free from yellow fever. "*Similia Similibus Curantur.*"— C. N.

These sudden and complete cures in so large a number were certainly a new feature presenting itself to our observation. The entire removal of remittent, as well as yellow fevers, by means of any treatment, although we do not pretend to call it impossible, is still a very rare occurrence. On the other hand, it is more common to see the fever progressively increased by any violent treatment. He quotes some authors who maintain the possibility of arresting the progress of the disease by bleedings and other means. Such are Thomas,* O'Halloran,† Catel.‡ The father of medicine observed that the progress of acute diseases could be arrested by bleedings. It is a pity, says Houdart,§ that he never thought of doing so.

---

* "Fièvre Jaune d'Amerique." Paris, 1823, p. 82.
† "Aperçu Succinct de la Fièvre Jaune." Paris, 1824, p. 105–8.
‡ Chervin, "Identité," &c., (Bulletin de l'Acad., T. VII., p. 1114.
§ "Etudes sur Hippocrate." 2me Edition. Paris, 1840.

If Fuster remarks that he has never been able to arrest the winter fevers of the Torrid Zone, he only admits the insufficiency of his therapeutic method.

But, continues Manzini, in the case of the inoculated, it was not a progressive diminution—a slow killing of the fever—which we observed; it was a complete destroying of it (jugulation), in the whole force of the word, as we have never observed it with the unacclimated, in consequence of which five hundred and eighty cases of fever, which had manifested themselves with all the violence of yellow fever, were promptly reduced to the proportions of simple ephemeral or prolonged fever. This result was owing to the inoculation. It furnished to Manzini's mind the method by which he could calculate the proportion according to which the unacclimated arrived at the point of complete acclimation under the influence of this operation.

There is also a fact which corroborates his view: this was the absence of all ephemeral fevers in former years at the Military Hospital. On the other hand, Manzini quotes numerous authorities, according to whom there marches along with the regular yellow fever epidemic one of a more ephemeral and milder character.

The truth with regard to this question may be stated as follows: The first attack of fever is generally the most severe and dangerous. The ephemeral form seems sometimes sufficient to harmonize the constitution with the new climate, although very often it indicates that the subject will have very rude and frequent attacks to submit to before he arrives at this result.

In resuming, Manzini proclaims the following incontestible fact, *that inoculation serves the same purpose as acclimation.*

These generally ephemeral and sometimes remittent fevers were, according to his conviction, modified yellow fevers, which on no consideration ought to have been separated from the 70 cases which did not present the characteristic hæmorrhage. For, notwithstanding this fact, the committee had classed them among the 121 cases of yellow-fever, and by the side of the 51 affected with the hæmorrhages.

The moment has now arrived to demand the cause of such exclusion, and to demonstrate that nothing could authorize the admission of the 70 cases to be considered as yellow fever, to the exclusion of the 580 of which the committee took no notice whatever.

Is it, Manzini asks, because the majority of these cases have only lasted five days? That could not be the case, because Mr. Bastareche has pronounced the case of General Concha to be yellow fever (in the *Gaceta de Habana*), although it lasted only twenty-four hours.

If they pretend to diagnosticate the disease by the number of days elapsed, the case of an inoculated lady may be mentioned, which the president of the commission, Mr. Gutierrez, pronounced to be yellow fever, which was restored in five days. Subsequently, the lady was again attacked, and died of the disease.

In resuming, it may be mentioned that the 701 cases of fever among the inoculated were all cases of yellow fever, if we admit that the diagnosis can be established without having recourse to the hæmorrhage characterizing it. In the contrary case, there were only 51 cases, of which 47 died.

DIAGNOSIS.

After innumerable quotations from all the writers on yellow fever, Manzini asks the significant question: What are the definite characteristic diagnostic symptoms of yellow fever? All the authors answer him that the jaundice and black vomiting constitute the *l'étendard* or the signals of yellow fever, just as the bubo and partial mortification form those of the plague.

Very truly he says: Of what advantage is it to characterize a fever in its initiatory stage with a phenomenon which only appears at its close? The same remark applies to another phenomenon—the jaundice—which only begins to appear on the third or fourth day.

In this way you could not diagnosticate the fever until the third or fourth day, because these signs do not commence to appear before that time. Finally, the icterus appears, and then it is said, this is yellow fever.

Is that so certain, continues Manzini; has not Bontius proved that it accompanies all acute maladies in the Torrid Zone?[*] Savaresi, has he not affirmed the same after him?   (p. 76.)

Pouppé has observed it at Saint Domingo in the double tertian (VI., p. 44). Campet has observed it in Cayenne, as generally characteristic of the same disease, and has seen it twice appear in the rare form of a complete yellowness (pp. 126, 130, 136). Savaresi

---

[*] " Med. Ind.," Chap. X.

has observed it in Martinique, in remittent, intermittent, and nervous fevers (p. 251). M. Catel in the intermittents of this same Antilles.* M. Rochoux, at Guadeloupe, in the gastric inflammatory fever.† Dr. W. Parry in the remittent fever. M. G. Douglas Dods has made the same observation at Demerara, in the same way as Drs. Damill and Edw. Bradford have in several of the Antilles of the western coast of Africa.‡ Mr. Levacher, finally, has observed it in the double tertian of St. Lucia (p. 130).

Wherever yellow fever prevails epidemically, no doubt jaundice is often present; but, in order to come to the truth with regard to its diagnostic value, we must mention that certain physicians consider it an uncertain unreliable pathognomonic symptom. Of this number are Lind,§ Arejula (p. 184), Gilbert (p. 76), Pugnet (pp. 359, 380), Audonard (pp. 67, 68), Caillot (p. 176), Ranul,‖ Chabert (p. 13), Devize (pp. 34, 36), Andévol (p. 116), Dariste (p. 134), Levacher (p. 88), and Moreau de Jonnès.

Manzini is of opinion that yellow fever is best characterized by hæmorrhages, *sui generis;* but, as he himself confesses that this phenomenon is not present in the slighter cases, we come to the inevitable homœopathic conclusion that the whole *ensemble* of all the

---

* Chervin, " Bulletin de l'Academic de Méd.," Vol. VII., p. 1110.
† " Rech. sur la Fièvre Jaune," pp. 221, 251.
‡ " Second Rapport," pp. 320, 328, 331, 340.
§ " Mal. des Européens." Paris, 1785. Vol. I., p. 171.
‖ Mr. O'Halloran. pp. 205, 206.

symptoms constitute the true characteristic of yellow fever.*

The above facts show that there exists a strong resemblance between the intermittent, remittent, and other fevers of tropical climates; that, in fact, they are only manifestations in different degrees of the same miasmatic virus. The same homœopathic remedies will subdue them.

Finally, the work winds up with a severe criticism of Mr. Bastareche's report to the Government. This gentleman, it seems, has not done justice to the inoculation, as has been pretty clearly established by the minute analysis of his report.

If we again impartially review Mauzini's whole account of the inoculation, we must come to the conclusion that it has in some measure been successful.

This whole question deserves our most serious consideration, and we particularly call upon all physicians, who have the opportunity, to investigate the action of Crotalus in epidemic yellow and malignant bilious fevers. It is only after repeated trials that we can arrive at a final solution of the subject.

---

* Mr. Claude Bernard, in his "Lectures on Experimental Pathology," makes the following observation: "We must bear in mind that a disease is not characterized by a single symptom; it consists rather of a complete series of symptoms, standing to each other in the relation of cause and effect."—C. N.

NINE NEW CASES

REMITTENT FEVER.

I. Miss M. S., aged twenty-two, was afflicted in the summer of 1861 with a bilious remittent fever, which was cured in a few days by the administration of Crotalus Horridus 3, in water, a teaspoonful every two hours. She received no other remedy. Crotalus acted like a charm. The symptoms, as I noted them down at the time, were the following: chilliness, alternately with heat; occasionally sudden cold perspiration; pulse full, and 100 in a minute. The eyes were sunk, with a dark-brown ring surrounding them; tongue dry in the centre, and yellow; the point red; constant vain efforts to evacuate the bowels; nausea and sick stomach. The passages are only slight, of a black color, and pappy consistence; soreness in chest and stomach; pain on touching them. She cannot lie on the left side. Great drowsiness all the time, and excessive weakness.

II. Mrs. O., aged seventy-one. Has two paroxysms of fever every day, with the pulse 120. (The administration of Crotalus brings the pulse down to a 100 on the first day.) The disease had lasted six weeks, and although various remedies were resorted to, Crotalus-horridus 3, in water, always had the best effect. The following symptoms were the most prominent; skin dry, afterwards cold perspiration; very thirsty; takes a little water at a time; burning heat on top of the head; heat in both cheeks, with redness; light-headed; eyes sunk;

tongue coated yellow, and dry; bitter taste in mouth; soreness and dryness of throat, which presents a dark-red appearance; hawking up of greenish yellow phlegm, with sweetish taste; sick stomach after eating, with vomiting and purging, slight pain in the region of the liver; dark-brown diarrhœa; wakefulness. This disease was entirely cured by Crotalus-horridus, aided by Baptisia-tinctoria.

After having the disease so severely, it returned a year afterwards in a milder form, and was cured by the same remedy. The symptoms were very similar, with the exception of a cough, which was cured by Laurocerasus.

III. A homœopathic physician in the country reported to me the following case of bilious vomiting, which was entirely cured by Crotalus in the 5th dilution. The case was of thirteen weeks standing, and had been given up by the old school. Symptoms: *She could not lie on the right side nor back without instantly producing dark-green vomiting;* soreness in the back part of the head, on pressure, worse on motion or sitting up in bed; drawing in the right side of the head, worse after eating, and producing great dizziness in the back part of the head. She sleeps only in the middle of the night, after which she feels better. She feels sick if she sleeps in the daytime. Light hurts the eyes, and everything looks yellow, (at first everything looked blue to her). Aching in the liver; great heaviness in the stomach, with vomiting of everything she eats in the morning. She can eat better in the afternoon, and she feels sometimes as if she could eat fat pork. A continual acid taste on the tongue; inclined to be constipated; menses too early, and too sparse; they are dark at first; roaring in the ears; great numbness of arms and legs, with coldness at times; skin very dark-brown. After the first dose of Crotalus 5, she vomited but once, and was able to be out of bed in one week.

IV. Mrs. M. S., aged sixty-nine, was cured in a few days, by Crotalus 3, of a severe bilious fever, with the following symptoms: Chills in feet and hands, followed by heat in the head, which ached before; mouth dry; very thirsty; foul breath; heat and redness in the right cheek; on closing eyes, wandering of mind; yellowish color of the face; sensation of excoriation of the stomach, with soreness of touch; complete want of appetite; eructations of wind; *gnawing aching pain in the liver*; sanguinolent discharges from the bowels. In addition to the above she was also afflicted with hepatization of the right lung, and consequent shortness of breath, always expectorating much yellow phlegm, after severe hard cough, and soreness on the left side. The effect of the Crotalus was assisted by the exhibition of Baptisia-tinctoria. The cough was cured by cod-liver oil.

V. Lieutenant W., of Commodore Wilkes' expedition, consulted me, quite lately, in his case of yellow fever, which he had contracted on the coast of Cuba. Although much diminished in violence, it never ceased entirely, notwithstanding numerous powerful remedies had been exhibited for six weeks, until he took the Crotalus-horridus 3, in water. In two days after, a slight aggravation, the fever was arrested. He considered this effect so remarkable that he mentioned it to everybody. In order to break the fever, he had received Quinine in thirty grain doses, repeatedly, also Calomel. Finally, Nitro-muriatic-acid, but without avail. He did not improve until he reached a colder latitude, and his fever was not arrested until he took the Crotalus.

VI. Miss V. Headache with high fever, mostly at night, with great drowsiness; aching in all the bones; heat in forehead; the slightest motion hurts the head; burning in the chest. Crotalus-horridus 2, cured, after Aconite and Belladonna had been administered in vain.

VII. Mr. M., went with the volunteers into Maryland, and was encamped on a small stream. Returning soon after he was attacked with a bilious fever, with the following symptoms. Bilious vomiting, with violent fever and delirium, entire forgetfulness of everything; dullness of the head with great apathy and fretfulness; everything tastes bitter, and sometimes acid; finally, very fœtid diarrhœa; tongue dark brown; constant drowsiness; dryness of the skin; (for these last three symptoms Crotalus is particularly indicated,) urine high-colored. When the crisis took place after Crotalus, there was a warm perspiration. Two days after commencing the Crotalus the brown color from the tongue gradually disappeared, and he had several green watery passages, always a very favorable symptom for the speedy cure of these fevers.

VIII. Mr. A. M. Chilliness every afternoon; a kind of crawling up and down the back, and afterwards all over, for five or six hours: severe pressure on the top of the head, running to the ears, with light-headedness and confusion, and heat from the head to the feet; shooting pain from the occiput down the spine and arms; foul breath; tongue coated yellow; bitter taste in the mouth, and nausea; soreness to the right side of the pit of the stomach, through to the shoulders; aching in the middle of the chest, to the back; dull pain across the hips, and also in the back and left shoulder; constant inclination to stool, with dark-brown blackish discharges. Crotalus 3, at once cured all these symptoms.

IX. Dr. W. Jackson Simon of Philadelphia, reported to me the following case of a cure of bilious fever with Crotalus, which I will give in his own words:

Having lost my notes, taken during the illness of Mr. Wm. W., I will have to depend on my memory for a statement of his case. Oct. 5, 1860, was this day requested to visit Mr. Wm. W., aged twenty-eight years. Constitution remarkably good. Had never been sick, until two months previous, at which time he was in the West, and had fever and ague. Temperament bilious sanguine. I found him complaining of severe frontal headache, and alternate chills and heat. Tongue furred white, the tip and edges scarlet red, pulse full and strong, about 140 per minute. Complained of some soreness of the abdomen on pressure, but none when that was removed. I prescribed Aconite and Rhus-tox., for some time, but without any improvement. Other remedies were given as the symptoms indicated, but all failed to relieve him. On the 21st day of my attendance, finding the patient much worse, I called Dr. J. G. Howard in consultation. We used a number of remedies, but without any apparent benefit. His condition at this time was as follows: tongue dry and cracked; dark-brown streak down the centre: the edges of a deep red color; occasional bilious discharges; no appetite; a cold clammy perspiration on the forehead and temples; skin yellow. Would speak when roused by shaking, seemed entirely unconscious of everything. Urine of a dark-red color, depositing a dark yellowish red sediment. Pulse 50, weak.

As his mother was a widow, and he her only son, I felt extremely anxious to save his life. While on a visit to Mr. Radde's store to purchase medicines, a new work was handed me, "On Crotalus in Fevers," by Dr. Neidhard. In glancing over it, I saw several cases given, corresponding in symptoms to Mr. W's case, in which the author had used Crotalus with great success. I asked Mr. Radde if he had any that was reliable. He said no, but thought he could get some from a physician just from Havana. I waited about two hours when he returned with a drachm vial of the third trituration. I immediately returned to my patient, and informed his mother that I had something which I hoped would relieve him. If it did not, I could do nothing more. I left five powders containing one grain each, directing one to be given every three hours until all were taken. On my visit the next morning I found my patient conscious, and wanting something to eat. The medicine was continued every six hours, for three or four days, when the patient being able to sit up, it was discontinued. In ten days he was able to attend to his business.

In conclusion I will remark that I have since used this remedy in typhoid and bilious remittent fevers with marked success.

Malan's Family Guide.. — 30
  do   do   in Spanish .... — 75
Marcy, Homœopathy and Allopathy.......................... — 50
Marcy & Hunt's Theory and Practice, 2 vols 12 00
Materia Medica of American Provings 1 00
Metcalf, Homœopathic Provings............................ 1 50
Millard, Consumption .... — 75
  do   Guide for Emergencies....................... — 50
Minton, Diseases of Women and Children................... 3 50
Morgan on Indigestion, Constipation, &c................... — 75
Munde on Scarlet Fever.................................... — 50
Mure's Materia Medica..................................... 1 00
Neidhard on Crotalus Horr. in Yellow Fever............... — 75
  do   on Diphtheria (in press) ....
New Provings of Cistus can, Cobaltum, Zingiber, &c........ — 75
North American Journal of Homœopathy, per volume 4 00
Oehme, Domestic Physician................................ — 60
Peters on Headaches and Diseases of the Head 3 00
  do   Apoplexy.. 1 00
  do   Diseases of Females and Married Females......... 1 50
  do   Diseases of Married Females 1 00
  do   Principal Diseases of the Eyes.................. 1 50
  do   Internal   do   do 1 00
  do   Diseases of the Brain.......................... 1 00
  do   Nervous Derangements........................... 1 00
  do   Principles and Practice of Medicine............ 3 50
Practical Guide.. — 20
Pulte's Domestic Physician................................ 3 00
  do Woman's Medical Guide........................ 1 50
Philadelphia Journal of Homœopathy, 4 vols., bd........... 8 00
Rapou on Typhoid Fever................................... — 50
Ran's Organon 1 25
Rell on Aconite... — 75
Rokitansky, Pathological Anatomy .... — 75
Rueckert, Therapeutics.................................... 4 00
Ruoff's Repertory... 1 50
Rush's Veterinary... — 50
Schaefer's Veterinary Homœopathy........................ 2 00
Sharp's Tracts, 12 numbers................................ — 75
Small's Diseases of the Nervous System................... 1 00
  do   Homœopathic Practice.......................... 3 00
  do   do   do German Edition.................... 3 00
  do   Pocket Manual.................................. — 40
  do   do   German Edition..................... — 40
Stapf's Additions to the Materia Medica................... 1 50
Tarbell, Homœopathy Simplified........................... 1 25
  do   Sources of Health............................. — 50
Ten Reasons for Preferring Homœopathy................... — 05
    do   do   do   German Edition.............. — 10
Tessier on Asiatic Cholera................................ — 75
  do   on Pneumonia................................. — 75
Teste, Diseases of Children............................... 1 50
Vanderburgh, Appeal for Homœopathy...................... — 15
Williamson, Diseases of Females and Children............. 1 00
Wolf on Apis-Mellifica.................................... — 25

PERIODICALS.

North American Journal of Homœopathy, quarterly,...........per year $4 00
Hahnemanian Monthly...................................... 3 00

www.ingramcontent.com/pod-product-compliance
Lightning Source LLC
Chambersburg PA
CBHW032201010726
47493CB00008BA/2783